Finish Line

Juanita Kees

Finish Line

Published by Juanita Kees (Kees2Create)

ISBN: 978-0-6456319-0-6

Cover Design Copyright © by Paradox Book Cover Designs

Dear Reader

t's taken 7 long years to polish this book. I've rewritten it so many times, convinced it was absolute rubbish. It's had more rejections and swipe-lefts than most dating sites, so thank you for swiping right.`

I would like to say a special thank you to my critique partners, beta readers and amazing proofreader for picking up the things I could no longer see. Also a very big thank you to my readers for motivating me to keep on writing. Without you all, this story would still be gathering dust in the drawer.

I am a huge fan of car racing and have written the track scenes from a great deal of research, so please forgive any technical errors. All mistakes are my own and I've used a fair bit of artistic license to make them as realistic as possible.

I hope you enjoy Isadora and Carmelo's journey to a happy-ever-after. They've worked hard for it, so please be kind when you review them.

Blessings to you all,

Juanita Kees

Chapter One

Carmelo Iannello stood at the office window, looking out over the view of the Bay, his white shirt pressed to perfection and his Armani trousers tailored to fit his tall frame. San Francisco's most eligible bachelor had women young and old swooning at his feet. Isadora studied him thoughtfully. She wouldn't be one of the many notches on his bedpost.

As the CEO of *Fit to Race*, he'd grown his race and gym wear franchise from a small on-line store to a world-wide sensation. Gym-goers, race fans, drivers, pit crew, and track girls scrambled to buy the sought-after range, making him a billionaire.

Tanned skin spoke not only of his exotic heritage, but also of the playboy who spent many sunlight hours enjoying the open waters on his luxurious sixty-foot, eighteen-million-dollar yacht. Today though, he was all about business.

"When you're ready, would you take notes, please, Sara?"

The name slipped from his lips in a way that made her skin heat and her mind want to forget her true identity. Sara Stewart was a lie, a disguise that hid Isadora de la Cruz from public scrutiny.

He turned to lean casually against the window ledge, the movement drawing her gaze below the waistband of those perfectly tailored trousers.

Isadora glanced down at her digital tablet; stylus poised to take notes like the efficient personal assistant she'd been employed to be. Inserting herself into that role came easier these days, although she missed the adrenaline of her real job.

The thrill of the race, the headiness of a win, and the cool kiss of metal on her fingertips as she held the trophy over her head. This man, who oozed sex appeal, had stolen that satisfaction from her. She'd do well to remember that.

"Enjoying the view, Ms. Stewart?" A smile tugged at his lips.

"I'd say you're fortunate to have the best view of the Bay in San Francisco." Isadora ignored his smug innuendo. He'd be used to catching women admiring the generous assets his heritage had bequeathed him with. She adjusted her grip on the stylus. "Depends on one's tastes, of course. Views can be disappointingly deceptive. Ready to take notes when you are."

Isadora waited until he'd moved to sit behind his desk before she risked a glance at his face. Carmelo could not be termed a classically handsome man. His features were too sculptured for that. But there was something about his face and the way he moved that made him irresistibly sexy and difficult to ignore.

Perhaps it was the confidence in his stride, or the pride he carried so easily on his shoulders. Whatever it was, she'd felt the burn of attraction ever since she'd met him in the flesh. Which was a shame because he owed her – big time. The sobering thought made her shift irritably in her seat, annoyance chasing away the lure of desire.

"Do you have somewhere more ... interesting ... to be, Ms. Stewart?" Full, sensual lips clamped down on her fake name as liquid brown eyes roamed her face.

Heat flushed up from the skin of her throat. According to office gossip, that mouth could do wicked things to a woman. "No, sir."

She had no desire to find out any time soon whether those rumors were true or not. Seeking revenge and answers through seduction was not on her agenda anytime soon.

She was here to uncover the truth, to extract a public apology from the Iannello empire and bring the great man himself to his knees for the humiliation he'd brought to her reputation. To expose him and Harlon Meira to the world for the liars they were. When he and his management team had accused her of ordering illegal modifications to the team car, she'd lost the job she lived for and her dreams.

Only when the truth came out, could she shed her Sara Stewart persona. Then the gossip tabloids would move on from the scandal that soured her racing record and reputation. Once she'd cleared her name, she would no longer need this job. She'd be free to move on and go back to doing what she really loved — NASCAR.

But before she could shed her Sara Stewart persona, Isadora had to find evidence of his involvement in the race scandal that had resulted in her being fired from his team.

"Ready when you are." She smoothed the vintage-style dress down over her hips and thighs and tucked the full skirt under her legs.

The movement caught his attention and he studied her from head to thigh with an intensity that had her fidgeting in her seat again. Desire roared around her body, lit by the unwelcome fuse of attraction.

Her heart ached knowing that this was the man who had destroyed her life, who had taken her dreams and trampled them underfoot. He didn't deserve to be so damn lust-worthy. Isadora avoided his gaze so he couldn't see the rising anger in her eyes.

"Right." He shifted forward in his seat and leaned

his elbows on the surface of his desk, his fingers creating a steeple. "Cancel my dinner date with Giovanna Esperanza. Send her flowers — white arum lilies."

"But … she hates arum lilies. They're a flower more suited to a funeral than a —" What did one call the beautiful Giovanna? A lover, a mistress? The woman the gossip rags were wagering on being Mrs Iannello? "... friend," she finished, the word lame on her tongue.

"Exactly. Ending a relationship is a bit like a funeral, is it not?"

Eyes wide, words tumbled out of her mouth. "You're breaking up with Giovanna Esperanza?" No one broke up with the supermodel, especially the one who'd made his *Race Girl* track wear famous. *She* broke up with *you*. "What about the fashion shoot for the winter launch?"

"Cancel it and put a hold on production."

Stunned, Isadora hesitated. "Are you sure?" Disbelief had her questioning his sanity. "The winter range has race fans everywhere excited. The orders are stacked sky high already. Canceling or putting the project on hold would cost the company a fortune in pre-order refunds." Far higher a penalty than the fine he'd paid to the racing tribunal for cheating at Daytona Beach. Had the great Carmelo Iannello lost his freaking mind?

"You dare to question my decision, Sara?"

Isadora shrugged off the cold sting of horror. "I'm

not your business advisor, Mr Iannello, I'm your secretary. I'm simply surprised that you would make such an expensive call." His knee-jerk decision that might cause his multi-billion-dollar empire to crumble should have made her happy. "The media will have a field day dragging your name through the mud." Exactly as he had done hers. She tapped in a list of things required to stop the project, the magnitude of the task ahead and the fallout from it seeping into reality. "This line of attire was set to change the whole fashion face of the racing world."

"You disapprove."

"It's professional suicide." Isadora looked up and caught his frown. "I'm sorry if I've overstepped the mark, sir, but a lot of work has gone into the project already. We've hired more staff, ordered new factory equipment, the materials, the cost … I don't understand …"

"How long have you worked for me?"

"Sorry?" His question threw her off guard. Was he about to fire her for being upfront? She'd worked too hard at her disguise, waited too long for revenge to lose this job just yet. Isadora wanted to be the one to leave, to destroy his world and crush his dreams, the way he had hers.

It was bad enough that he'd almost caught her out two days ago when she'd found the pit crew's maintenance file in the cabinet. She'd been so close to finding at least a very small piece of the evidence she needed to prove that he'd ordered the illegal modifications to her car. But he'd walked out of his office as Isadora was about to open the manilla folder, and she'd had to file it away again.

Drawing her attention back to him, he repeated the question. "How long have you been my assistant, Sara?" He arched an eyebrow, waiting for a response, eyes full of amusement, lips tilted in a smile that made her want to trace them with her fingertips. Her cheeks grew warm.

Damn him, why did he have the kind of face she wanted to touch? Thinking about how his skin would feel under her hands was pointless. Isadora cast a look at the calendar app on her notebook that counted out the days and hours since she'd been forced to leave the career of her dreams and settle for a desk job. "Three months, five days and fourteen hours."

"Not that you're keeping track." He grinned, and her resolve crumbled once more. His smile could melt a damn iceberg. "That's longer than most of my assistants have lasted."

Where was he going with this? She'd always remained professional even when she'd caught herself daydreaming about him between silk sheets, all twisted bodies and naked skin, torn between wanting him and despising him at the same time. Why torment her heart and mind with fantasies that could never be fulfilled?

No matter how much Isadora hated him for what he'd done, that didn't mean he hadn't crept into her dreams for entirely different reasons.

"You might as well have counted minutes and seconds too. Am I such a monster to work for that you need to count the months, days, and hours?" Carmelo rose from behind the desk and strolled around it, moving closer, his intense gaze never leaving her face.

Isadora shifted against the unwanted desire that look brought to her blood. She dragged her mind back to his question, willing her traitorous body to behave. "My opinion of you doesn't come into play. You're my employer. I was raised to treat my superiors with respect and do the job I was employed to do."

"Respect. That's just the thing." He knelt beside the chair and looked up at her with eyes she could so easily get lost in. "Do people respect my name, my money, or me?"

"You've worked hard for all three, sir." Despite all the damage he'd done to her reputation, she couldn't deny that he'd earned every dime he'd worked for at *Fit to Race*.

His smirk appeared a touch cynical. "But the first two outweigh the last, my dear Sara. Tell me, if there was no money, no glamor, no name ... would people like the real Carmelo Iannello?"

A bubble of nervous laughter built in her throat. Was he serious? This man-god crouched at her side with his expensive suits, engaging looks and a voice like warm caramel sauce was worried no one liked him? "Why wouldn't they?"

"Because they don't know him at all." With a sigh, he pushed up out of the crouch. The movement pulled his pants tight across muscular thighs. "You know nothing about me, and I know nothing about you."

Well, now that wasn't entirely true. She knew him too well, especially the playboy mantle he wore like a crown and the havoc he could wreak with a simple command.

"You don't have to know me, Mr Iannello, as long as you're happy with the job I do. My opinion of you doesn't count. It's not like we're friends who mix in the same circles." Whatever was going on in his mind, she wanted no part of it. No matter what her heart felt, or how her body reacted to him, her mind was set on payback. "If that's all for now, I'll get onto the production department to cancel the orders in the system and arrange for marketing to prepare a press release for the media."

He reached down to tangle his finger in the blonde curls that had fallen forward over her shoulders, giving one a little tug. "You have beautiful hair." The smooth, warm touch of his fingers grazed her cheek as he let the curl slip away. "You should always leave it loose. I think I'd like to get to know you better, Sara."

For goodness sake, this had gone on long enough. If

she listened to anymore of what he was dishing out, she'd melt into a puddle at his feet and agree to anything he asked for. Parts of her already confirmed the melting process was well and truly underway, but this flirtation — and whatever else it was he had up his ass today — had to end. Now. His HR department would have a crisis on their hands if she mistook his gesture for harassment, except the only one having naughty thoughts at his touch would be her.

"I keep my personal and professional lives separate, Mr Iannello. We don't play in the same league." Or even the same ballpark. Isadora pushed the curls back over her shoulder, dislodging his hand as she stood.

Even in three-inch heels, she barely topped his shoulder. Attraction pulsed between them, the material of her skirt brushing his pants as she sought space to move, trapped between him and the chair. He stood too close, the scent of his cologne reaching in to embrace her senses — something spicy, sexy, and evocatively exciting.

Isadora pictured him naked after a shower — all six feet and a few inches of him — solid, tanned muscle. No doubt he'd dab that stuff in places wherever his pulse could deliver a shot of pure temptation with every heartbeat. Men wearing cologne had always been her downfall, weakened her knees, and oh Lord, she was tempted to taste him right now.

"Excuse me, Mr Iannello. If we're going to stop

production of the clothing line, I've got a lot of work to do."

She kept her eyes on the top button of his shirt where his tie sat a little off-center. Isadora wanted to straighten it — no, wait — rip it off and tear open those buttons to get her hands on the skin underneath. But if she did that, she'd be just like any other woman who'd fallen for his brand of charm. Falling for his body was bad enough, falling for his charm would be career-ending fatal. And he'd already fired her once.

"Of course," he said, moving aside. "I stand corrected. You are right. I have overstepped the line, and I apologize."

With a glance up at his face, she witnessed his mask of professionalism descend once more. Isadora stepped around him and headed for the door, relieved to put some distance between them.

"Sara?"

She shouldn't want to hear her real name fall from his lips. How would it taste on his tongue? Without turning around, Isadora closed her eyes and clutched the digital notebook tightly against her breasts. "Yes, Mr Iannello?"

"I would like you to co-host a cocktail party with me tonight."

Reality snuck back in with a sharp, cold jab. There was no way in hell she could attend one of those parties on his yacht. The paparazzi loved them, splashing photos of his guests all over the pages of celebrity magazines. The risk of recognition would be way too high, especially if she knew any of the race models who might attend the event.

"Excuse me?" Isadora turned to find him staring out the window again.

"I need a hostess."

"I'll consult your list of contacts and arrange it."

"No. I want *you*."

She shivered against the emphasis and the visions his request brought to mind. The ultimate cost of a moment's distraction would be exposure before she could extract revenge. "I have other plans ..." *Yeah, right. Plans to watch* Dirty Dancing *for the umpteenth time while you share popcorn with the cat.*

"Cancel them. My driver will collect you at 6.30 pm sharp. I'll pay you triple time in overtime for the effort if you attend."

The bonus would come in handy. It would contribute towards the lawyer's fees to prove she was innocent of race fixing. Maybe get her suspension from competing lifted so she could get back behind the wheel for the next NASCAR season.

And the cost to her heart? Everything. If Isadora wanted to extract every ounce of compensation from this man who'd stolen her dream, she couldn't allow herself to crumble under his charm. She had to ignore the exhausted slump of his shoulders, the tiredness in his face, and the plea in his voice.

"I'm sorry. The answer is no."

He dragged a hand over his features, pinched the bridge of his nose between his thumb and forefinger, as if he could drain away what bothered him by doing so. "Please?"

His quiet request had Isadora's resistance unraveling like the ribbon on a child's Christmas gift as she caved to the desperation in his tone. Carmelo Iannello *never* begged, ever. And maybe mingling with his friends and colleagues at the party would provide an opportunity to learn something more about what happened before the race that day. People tended to dish up dirt when they were drunk. What harm could it do to help him out?

Chapter Two

What the hell was he thinking? Carmelo raked a hand through his hair, annoyed and frustrated as Sara stood silent in the room. Messing with his assistant — especially a good one like Sara — was stooping to a whole new level of low, even for him.

But she'd sat there looking so damn hot in a dress that clung to her curves, and eyes the color of roasted chestnuts, reminding him of lazy, sensuous nights in front of a warm fire.

Beautiful, dangerous eyes that had looked right into his damn soul and stirred a passion in him he hadn't felt in a very long time. It was as if his personal assistant could see right through his mask.

Carmelo lost interest in the view of the Bay, looking at

Sara instead. A need for her built in him, one that had him wondering what it would be like to make love to her until his mind blanked out of this funk that possessed him. But it wouldn't be fair to Sara to use her to exorcise his demons.

"Why me?" Her question fell softly into the space between them, as she turned back to face him.

Carmelo took his time to answer. He'd noticed her interest, the spark between them. He'd felt her gaze rake his body as he'd stood at the window, every nerve end aware of her presence. He'd be a liar if he didn't admit to covertly admiring her curves on more than one occasion.

But this sweet, quiet Sara who went about her business looking after his. His reliable, stable employee who would carry out the mammoth task of canceling the production of race wear at his whim and deal with the fall out while restlessness tore at his gut.

A smile tugged at his lips. His assistant had been a quiet, unassuming presence in the office when needed. Somehow she'd snuck in under his skin and evolved into something more. He'd started to see the woman behind the stylus and notepad, and it scared him.

Her eyes searched his as she repeated her question. "Why me when you have a contact list full of more suitable companions for the night?"

"Because around you I don't have to pretend to be someone I'm not. You have a way of making me feel …

comfortable. Grounded in a way I've never been before."

"I'm not sure that's a compliment, or a good reason for me to act as your escort for the night. I don't mix business with pleasure."

"It's a compliment." He paced the distance between his desk and the window. "And the term *escort* doesn't suit you, Sara. It implies something you are most definitely not. I prefer *companion*. And I don't mean comfortable in the way of a favorite pair of slippers."

"Thank you. I think." Her eyebrows arched, her dry tone making his lips twitch.

"See? That's what I like about you. You're not afraid to say what you think around me. You treat me like a real person not a celebrity."

"Unfortunately for you, a man who achieves the top spot on the Forbes list of billionaires *is* a celebrity in the business world. It's a long fall from the pedestal you're on."

"And that's where so many have put me. On a pedestal. I find myself asking if this is the life I want after all." A billionaire playboy with a string of lovers who cared only that they'd snagged San Francisco's most eligible bachelor. "What is it like out there in the real world, Sara?"

She shifted on her feet, color seeping into her cheeks. "I'm not sure I'm the right person to ask."

"Do you have a family?"

"Not anymore." Sadness crept into her eyes. "It was only me and my dad for a long time, and now he's gone too."

"Tell me about him."

"He was my hero." A warm, reminiscent smile lit her face with affection. "We laughed a lot, argued sometimes, but he was always fair and just."

Something too close to jealousy twisted in his chest. "You were lucky to have at least one parent who loved you. My house … it echoes with loneliness." He hated going home to that. "My parents, they've been gone a very long time and I have no siblings. The only time I am truly happy is when I am out on the water, on the yacht or paddling the kayak through the swells in the Bay." And when Sara sat opposite him in that chair; sweet, undemanding, and beautiful.

"Then you should do what makes you happy." She clutched her digital notebook with one hand and smoothed her skirt with the other.

What would make him happy would be to bury himself in Sara's soft curves and forget about Giovanna's hard edges. He stepped away from the window to pour a drink, needing something to occupy his hands to stop him from reaching for her.

Tossing back two fingers of good whiskey, he silently scoffed at his reflection in the mirror above the bar. The women who moved in his circles knew the rules and how to play the game, but not Sara. He should withdraw his ridiculous invitation, call the whole thing off. That would be the wise thing to do.

The phone rang, rattling the silence that had fallen in the room.

Sara tapped her hands-free headset to answer, pausing a moment before saying, "I'm sorry, Miss Esperanza, but Mr Iannello is in a meeting at the moment." She winced and moved the earphones back from her ears as the sound of Giovanna's voice shrieked through the air.

"I am his girlfriend. His future wife. He will take calls from me, and I don't need some office *guard dog* telling me otherwise!"

Every nasty word reached Carmelo's ears and the discomfort that showed on Sara's face stung his heart. She was only following orders to screen his calls. Well, screw Giovanna. There'd be no parting gifts for her. Bad behavior would no longer be rewarded.

"Miss Esperanza, I'm really sorry. I can take a message for him if you like?"

"*Perciò fottiti, puttana*! You put him on the phone right now! He's not answering his cell phone and I want to speak to him."

With a hand on Sara's shoulder, he plucked the headset from her head, put it on, and said into the microphone, "And you eat with that mouth?"

Stunned silence drifted down the line before Giovanna gathered her wits to answer, "Darling! Why are you not answering your phone? I've been thinking about you all day, but your little secretary won't let me talk to you."

Her lips would be pouting around her words. There was a time when he would have kissed and nipped that pout away, but now it left him cold. Sara deserved an apology, but first he had to take care of his mistakes.

"That's because I don't want to talk to you. It's over, Giovanna. We're done."

"You're dumping me? *Bastardo! Sei ... un codardo del cazzo*!"

"Enough." The word came out on a growl. Stunned silence echoed down the line. "I'll be in touch with your agent. The photo shoot is canceled." He looked down at Sara, her eyes on his face. "And for the record, Giovanna, you were never in the running to be my wife."

The weight of his words found their target, the strike of realization echoing in her gasp. Her career with *Fit to Race* was over, her future as Mrs Giovanna Iannello in ruins. She tried begging, pleading, tears and threats. He hung up on the tirade of insults and threw the headset on the desk.

"Are you okay?" Carmelo squeezed Sara's shoulder gently.

She shrugged away his hand. "I'm fine. Giovanna might not be though. You might want to have someone check on her later."

The wall he'd built around his heart crumbled a little. It said a lot about Sara that she would put a heartless social climber like Giovanna first. Giovanna certainly wouldn't afford her the same respect. "I'll have her agent call around at her apartment. I handled that all wrong, didn't I?"

"A little. You shouldn't have strung her along if you had no intention to follow through."

The sting of anger in her tone found its target square in his chest. "I had no idea she was planning our wedding. I prefer the bride wait to be asked first." He shuddered at the thought that Giovanna had been under the impression she stood a chance at making it to the altar with him. Marriage was way down the list on his agenda, unless he was sure he'd met the right woman. "But even before Giovanna's call, it was wrong of me to put you in the center of my dissatisfaction with the road my life is taking."

"Then perhaps it's time to take a good, long hard look at where you're heading." Her chin tilted as she pushed a wayward curl behind her ear.

The fiery flash of her eyes seared through him. It would be easy to drown in that sea of chestnut lava. What would it take to make those eyes burn with desire instead of anger?

Carmelo reached for her hand, the urge to hold her and keep holding her streaking through him. Out of character, yes. Embracing someone outside of the bedroom led to a closeness — a bond — he preferred to avoid. In fact, even in bed, he preferred to avoid pro- longed body contact.

Risking at least a slap to the face, he gave in to the need to tug her close. The weight of her hair slid like silk against his skin as he placed his other hand at the back of her neck. Loosely, so she had room to pull away if she wanted to.

Her breasts grazed his shirt, her warm comfort penetrated his skin. Rigidly angry, she didn't move away, but instead held his gaze. Her lips only inches away, he wanted to kiss her until every ounce of frustration left them both.

"You're right. Change is way overdue. I am truly sorry, Sara." His thumb stroked the smooth skin of her cheek, soothing some of the tension from her spine.

She released a long, breathy sigh, her breasts brushing his chest. He wanted to gather her closer, burrow into her so their bodies aligned. The old Carmelo would have taken advantage. Hell, the new Carmelo wanted to take advantage, but his conscience called for caution. He didn't understand this sudden, all- consuming need for Sara, so he resisted the temptation and relaxed his grip on her.

"Take the rest of the day off. Marketing can deal with everything. I'll see you tonight."

"About tonight ... I can't ..." she began.

Carmelo pressed a forefinger to her lips, absorbed

their protest. "Help me out. Just this once. Tonight's celebration is for my good friend, Tony. A birthday party I've committed to, and even though I'm not exactly in a partying mood today, I'm reluctant to cancel on a friend."

What he needed was a distraction, a deterrent for the women who would descend on him, clamoring for his attention and a shot at bedding San Francisco's most eligible bachelor.

Having Sara's steady presence there would get him through. Yes, his PA was the safest choice. She had no demands on his body — a fact that shouldn't disappoint him the way it did. "I'll double my offer."

Her palm met his chest, fingers splayed as she pushed him back a step. "I'm not for sale." She turned and walked away; her stride determined.

Carmelo admired the way her dress clung to her shape, how the skirt caressed her legs, and he wished his arms didn't feel so cold and empty now she'd left his space. What reasonable explanation could he give for this need for her presence, to be close to her?

"Tell me, Sara, what do you see when you look at me?" He waited as she slowly turned back at the door to study him.

"I see a man with talent and power. When used incorrectly, those gifts can be dangerous ... destroying."

"You think I'm dangerous?"

Her nose tilted higher. "I think you're ruthless in pursuit of what you want."

"I'm a businessman. One doesn't become successful by sitting back and letting opportunities pass by. I need to be ruthless."

"There's a difference between being ruthless and being relentless."

Relentless. That was a word that said everything about his life. He shoved his hands into the pockets of his trousers. "Would you think less of me if I told you that I started from nothing? How I built an empire out of the rags I collected on the streets? That before I made it big, I was nothing more than a homeless street kid, caving to gang peer pressure to survive. The very people who refused me food or money on the streets back then are quite happy to attend the functions of the rich playboy I represent in this world today."

Her heart softened a little towards him. "I didn't know that. There's not much information about your background out there, only your success."

"I'd like to keep it that way. Only three people know the truth about my past. My lawyer, my driver, and now you. People might not feel the same way about doing business with me if they knew I once ran the streets with gangs. Society is funny that way." Carmelo rocked back on his heels. "So you see, Sara, it's a survival choice. I've had to be ruthless to win in life and stay in the game."

"Even if winning comes at someone's else's cost?"

"That would depend on the competition." Carmelo wondered at the bitterness in her tone, but his cell phone buzzed, distracting him. "Excuse me a moment." He answered before placing the caller on hold. "A couple of hours tonight, that's all I ask." It would be nice to have someone *real* at his side, someone who didn't measure everything in dollars and dimes. Someone with a quick mind he could have a sensible conversation with.

Sara looked at him, her gaze serious. "I'll commit to a couple of hours, that's all. And … Carmelo?"

His name on her lips sent a pleasant shiver up his spine. "Yes, Sara?"

"I don't think any less of you because of where you came from. In fact, I admire you more for getting out and making a success in life. My dad came to America with nothing but a dream to follow, so I know how hard you had to work to see your vision come to reality." She offered him a tentative smile. "See you tonight."

"I look forward to it." Carmelo refused to stop the answering smile that settled on his lips as she walked out the door, closing it firmly behind her.

Chapter Three

W hat on earth had possessed her to say yes? Isadora rifled through her wardrobe for something to wear. In a moment of weakness, she'd allowed him to slip in under her defenses and agree to this crazy idea. If someone recognized her and Carmelo found out who she really was, the whole plan would be ruined.

Staying out of the spotlight would be near impossible. The gossip rags trawled the docks at society parties, waiting to snap a shot of celebrities letting their hair down. Even though she'd taken great care to be unrecognizable in her Sara-disguise, the risk of exposure ran high.

That unforgettable race win still played on the screen highlights at every race at the Daytona Beach track while the subsequent team disqualification continued to rattle tabloid cages. Constantly on the lookout for her, every sports journalist wanted the scoop on the story behind Isadora de la Cruz's disappearance from the racing scene.

How nice it would be to be herself again, the free spirit she used to be. These days every public space felt like a trap, every function a risk of discovery. Just once she'd like to let her hair down, to dance the night away.

What would it be like to dance with Carmelo? Bodies touching with each twist and turn of a rumba ... or salsa ... the craving between them.

Isadora thrust the fantasy aside and stepped into the shower, letting the cool water stream over her. Fantasies were for dreamers, and she had no time to waste on daydreaming in trying to clear her name. It would be nice to not have to look over her shoulder to see who was watching, but she couldn't. Not until she'd proved her innocence.

Finishing up, she toweled off and slipped on her robe. Face scrubbed free of cosmetics, with her dyed blonde hair dark, wet, and straight, the real woman behind the disguise looked back at her from the mirror glass. Would Carmelo like Isadora de la Cruz if he got to know her? The risk taker, the speed demon, the ruthless competitor ... the woman?

With a sigh, she dried and curled her hair, reapplied her make-up disguise, and stepped into her cocktail dress. It didn't matter whether he liked her or not, as long as no one recognized her.

A spritz of Chanel on her pulse points, a pair of kitten-heeled pumps, and Sara Stewart was ready when Carmelo's driver pulled up outside her apartment building at the top of Lombard Street. If anyone asked how a personal assistant came to live in some of the most expensive real estate in San Francisco, she'd tell them she shared the apartment. No one needed to know her flat mate was a cat.

"Good evening, Sara," Joe greeted, opening the car door for her.

"Hey, Joe." Isadora grinned at him before sliding onto the plush, buttery leather of the back seat.

He slid back behind the wheel, pulled away from the curb, and negotiated the steep switchbacks. Lombard Street reminded her of a racetrack with the tight curves and bends. They needed control and concentration to negotiate, like her own life right now. One mistake, one over-steer, and everything could tumble downhill.

Joe's teeth flashed in a grin. "This is a surprise. You're not the usual style of passenger. Have you changed your mind about attending these functions?"

"No, I'm a stand-in tonight. Special favor for the boss. It's kinda short notice. Miss Esperanza ... won't be available for functions in future."

"Oh." Joe drew the word out, picking up on her hesitation and the underlying reason for Giovanna's lack of attendance. "Well, I guess there's another address to remove from the GPS."

Poor Joe. He would have seen many women come and go over the years. Isadora wondered how many discarded addresses he'd had to remove from his satellite navigation system. As a one-off arrangement with Carmelo, hers would now be one of them.

Joe turned on the radio and soft music filled the car. "Hmm, well you take care now, okay? Don't go falling for his charm or anyone else's. I'd hate to see you leave too."

Unease trickled up her spine. Joe had a point. She'd have to stay on her toes. She couldn't afford to blow her cover. If she stayed alert and stuck with her plan, there'd be no regrets. "I'll be fine."

As long as she could resist the enigma that was Carmelo Iannello. What was it about bad boys that attracted her even when she was fully aware of their sins?

The fifteen-minute drive to the exclusive St Francis Yacht Club off Marina Boulevard gave Isadora more time to think than she needed. This was a big mistake. Aside from the risk of her real identity being exposed, Joe was right. Carmelo wouldn't be the only threat there tonight. She'd have to do her best to avoid them all as much as possible. Meet and greet, make sure the food and drinks were being served and then leave as quickly as possible.

Did Carmelo really even need her there? He had staff for that. But there'd been a level of vulnerability in his tone she hadn't been able to ignore, and he'd offered her an unexpected opportunity to do a little scouting amongst his friends. There she could uncover his level of involvement in the scandal at Daytona Beach, something she'd failed to do so far at the office.

It wasn't like anyone would notice if she slipped away quietly later. The attention would be on the beautiful guests and the fanfare of an elite function. Hopefully, none of the models there tonight had doubled as track girls and any official photographers present were designated to runways rather than speedways.

The sun was setting in the Bay as they arrived in the car park at the yacht club. Fall was reputed to be the best time of year in San Francisco, and Isadora had to agree. The days were warm and sunny, and the nights mild and clear. In the summer months, fog often cloaked the Golden Gate Bridge, but now in late September it had cleared, and the view of the bridge against the backdrop of sunset was breathtakingly beautiful.

Joe pulled up alongside the pier and cut the motor. "You call me as soon as you're ready to go home. I won't be far away," he said, turning in his seat to face her.

Isadora drew the pashmina wrap around her shoulders. The chill would blow in off the water later and she'd be glad she'd worn it. "Thanks, Joe."

"No matter how late it is."

She smiled, pleased they'd forged a friendly acquaintance since Carmelo's transport arrangements often brought them in contact. "Of course, thank you."

Joe turned back in the seat and got out of the car. Coming around to the rear, he opened the door. Hands a little unsteady, Isadora smoothed the skirt of her dress.

"You look just fine. You've got this." Joe's reassurance did little to settle the flutter of nerves in her belly. "One of the crew will meet you at the end of the dock to take you out to where the yacht is anchored. Would you like me to walk with you?"

Isadora took a deep breath and let it out slowly. If only Joe knew the real reason for her nerves. One wrong move and everything she'd been working toward would be lost. "I'll be fine, thanks."

Joe chuckled. "Of course you will . You'll love the *Bay Princess*. She's a magnificent vessel. Take care now and have a little fun."

"See you later, Joe. Thanks for the ride."

"You're welcome."

He waved goodbye as Isadora stepped onto the wooden dock. Nerves rattled around under her rib cage as she approached the sleek motorboat waiting to transport her out to where Carmelo's mega yacht lay in the bay, a luxurious attestation of his success.

"Good evening, Ms. Stewart." The deckhand

assisted her into the seat beside him, his polo shirt proudly sporting the Iannello Group logo.

Isadora gripped the handrail as the motor engaged and a shot of adrenalin fizzed through her blood. She missed the exhilaration of speed and appreciated that the deckhand knew that the power of the boat's motor would be wasted on a slow chug.

She couldn't stop the silly grin from spreading or the laugh of enjoyment that escaped as the stern of the boat chased the swell and a frothy wake fanned out behind them. Too soon, the ride was over as they slowed to approach the yacht, Isadora's heart still pounding with excitement.

Carmelo stood at the port side rail with the breeze ruffling his jet-black hair. Her heart did a somersault that mirrored the one in her stomach. He'd unbuttoned his shirt, the material billowing around him as he leaned on the rail, the tension from the events of the day still apparent in the way he stood and the stiff set to his jaw.

Isadora's gaze travelled down the firm contours of his chest, his abdomen, and his waist. He'd removed the belt from his hips, and his pants rode them like a lover's hands.

Her pulse raced for an entirely different reason. The man should come with a warning label. It wasn't just his looks; it was the whole damn package. He might be a playboy, but she'd learned he was more than that in the short time she'd worked closely with him. He was a kind, generous, good boss who valued his staff, which was in total contrast to the man who had fired her from his racing team for something that wasn't her fault. The cost? Her career.

As a tough, savvy businessman he should have understood the price tag on the actions of his pit crew that day, yet it was Isadora who'd taken the fall. He hadn't even taken the time to see her himself, or ask what had happened that day, and she'd never got to meet the man who owned the team she'd raced for.

There were reasons for that, of course. Only team management got to hang out with the owner. Isadora was only one of the many drivers, no matter how good she was at her job or how many wins she'd had under her belt. The only reason she was on the team at all was because she'd come to it on Harlon Meira's recommendation. Perhaps the only thing she had to thank him for.

Harlon ... another man she wished to hell. An opportunistic bastard who'd lied to her as he'd emptied her bank account.

Carmelo's face drew her attention from the memory of the fool she'd been. Raw vulnerability lay in his expression as he watched the sunset. Whatever it was that occupied his thoughts pulled his mouth down at the corners and dragged at his shoulders. Something intangible that came from deep down inside him, a susceptibility she'd never seen before. Despite her own personal vendetta, it made her want to reach out and reassure him.

But she'd been down that road before. Fallen for a handsome face only to find that the person underneath was a fake. Harlon Meira had her fooled by the same charm and exotic good looks. Together they'd made a formidable racing team until she'd fallen for him. Only he'd conveniently forgotten to tell her he had a wife stashed away in Georgia.

Then came the scandal — the chassis adjustment violation — and the whole debacle was exposed; the affair, the illegal modifications to the race car, Isadora's disqualification from NASCAR racing and Carmelo's orders to fire her from the team. Branded as a race cheat, she'd lost everything. She couldn't forget that.

The motorboat slowed to a stop at the backboard and Carmelo moved from his spot at the rail to stroll toward them. Close up, his melancholy mood hinted at a sensitivity that made him human, approachable.

A flicker of hope lit in her heart. This invitation might not be a wasted opportunity after all. This softening in him might offer her the opportunity to at least save her reputation if not her career.

The weight of his gaze fell on her as the deckhand helped her aboard. Carmelo's fingers closed around hers. A flush crept through her to warm the chill of uncertainty from her bones.

"You came." A smile tipped his lips.

"Did you think I wouldn't?"

"Nothing in life is guaranteed."

Waves slapped against the hull as the motorboat sped back to the dock. Isadora stumbled against the sudden dip and sway as the movement tipped her against Carmelo, their bodies touching. A frisson of awareness raised goosebumps on her skin.

He slipped an arm around her waist to steady her, her hands landing on his naked chest. "Welcome aboard."

Sinew and toned muscle lay warm beneath her fingers. It wouldn't take much to imagine how it would feel to run her hands over the contours and allow her lips to follow their path.

He'd taste like spice and temptation, an intoxicating mix. Would his lips be warm and soft, or cold and hard, if he kissed her? The tightening of her body in response to the thought reminded Isadora of whose arms she was in and all the reasons she shouldn't be there.

"Thank you." She removed her hands from his chest and stepped back. "What time are your guests arriving? What do I need to do?" There, much safer ground. She breathed deeply to slow the erratic beat of her heart.

Carmelo chuckled and the deep sexiness of it almost made her forget all about breathing. "Relax, my staff has everything under control. Champagne?"

"I had no doubt they would which is why I'm not convinced I'm needed here."

"Yet still you came."

A waiter appeared from the cabin lounge with a bottle of *Dom Perignon* and two glasses on a tray. He poured the vintage *brut*, rich, and golden, infused with bubbles and topped with froth.

Carmelo lifted the glasses from the tray and the waiter melted away into the depths of the yacht. "Here's to providing me with moral support," he said, handing Isadora a glass. "There'll be questions about Giovanna and with you at my side, people will be less inclined to ask."

Isadora's fingers brushed his as she closed them around the delicate crystal stem of the champagne flute. The featherlight touch sent blood singing through her veins and curled her toes in the kitten-heeled pumps. Her gaze flew to his. Heat warmed his brown eyes.

Attraction tugged Isadora closer, licked at her belly, every nerve end on fire. His head descended to block out the sunset until all she could see was the glow of his skin. All she could smell was him, that unique scent that epitomized Carmelo Iannello — sex, sin, and heartbreak.

Even knowing his reputation and the need for self-preservation, she was powerless to stop those lips from taking hers because, God help her, she wanted to taste them so *damn* much.

Isadora put a hand on his chest to stop him, the warmth of his skin beneath her palm an invitation to explore. One she needed to ignore to put a stop to the madness — now.

"Mr Iannello —"

"Carmelo," he whispered, brushing his mouth over hers. Letting go of his hold on her champagne glass, he brought his hand up to cup her face, to draw her closer as his lips teased hers with languid kisses.

Her pulse pounded as his thumb stroked the sensitive skin behind her ear. He closed the gap between them, her only defense the champagne flute, now forgotten. The press of his hard length against her belly brought with it the need to feel it lower at the entrance to the part of her body that craved his attention.

Isadora's mind hazed over as her imagination took flight at the thought of them entangled together on silk sheets as he drove her over the edge of sanity with his big hands and beautiful mouth. The vision had her arching into him, satisfaction flowing through her at the growl he uttered against her lips.

His hand left her face to roam her curves, his fingers stroking out a hypnotizing rhythm against the material of her dress, the roll of his hips a tribute to his own need.

Insanity! The warning pounded through Isadora's head like a runaway train she was powerless to stop.

"Jesus, Sara," he bit out, tearing his mouth away from hers. Blowing out a long, unsteady breath, he tucked her head in under his chin, her ear to his chest against the pounding of his heart.

In the distance the roar of the motorboat engine announced the arrival of his guests. Carmelo released his hold with a gentle rub to her arms and stepped away. For a long moment he studied her, the burn of his assessment equaling the one that flushed her cheeks.

Reality descended with a dash of ice. Isadora took an unsteady sip of the champagne she'd almost forgotten she had in her hand. The rumors were true. He had a wicked mouth. And it couldn't happen again — no way — because unlike her fake persona, her attraction to Carmelo Iannello was dangerously real. She wasn't Sara Stewart, and she had no business enjoying kissing the enemy.

Chapter Four

*H*e should never have kissed her. Now the taste of her would linger on his tongue through the flavor of the champagne for the long night to come. She'd tasted as sweet and innocent as she'd looked, her response unrehearsed, instinctive and it had Carmelo wanting more.

Even now, as she patted her hair into place and straightened her dress, he wanted her in a way he'd never wanted a woman before.

Madness. He couldn't — wouldn't — have her. If he did, he'd risk losing the best damned assistant he'd had in favor of a night of lust-filled sex. Sara wasn't a player who deserved to be used and discarded like the soiled condom from a one-night stand.

Damned if he knew what it was that drove this need

for her but exploring it could only bring trouble. The further he stayed away, the better.

As the motorboat slewed to a stop and his friends boarded the yacht, Carmelo reached out to touch her fingers with his — a light brush when he really wanted to curl his hand around hers. "You okay?"

She smiled, the movement hesitant yet undeniably hot, and he wanted to possess that beautiful mouth all over again.

"All good."

Carmelo leaned a little closer, his lips brushing her ear. "I won't apologize."

"I'd be offended if you did."

"It won't happen again." Not that he didn't want it to because — *God damn it* — her mouth tasted like heaven.

She moved away as his friend, Tony strolled up the deck toward them. "It can't happen again."

The only problem with that was that now he'd tasted her, he was hooked. He wanted to invite her to his cabin where they could be alone to explore where the night would take them, but Tony was shaking his hand, ready to introduce the bevy of beauties he'd brought with him, and the moment was lost.

As guests poured aboard, his friends and acquaintances surrounded him. Sara's presence slowly melted away from his side. And there was another new experience for him. Usually, it never bothered him when his dates were swallowed up in the crowd, but tonight he caught himself looking over everyone's shoulders for a glimpse of Sara's blonde curls and the reassurance she was still there. What the hell was with that?

"A bit distracted tonight, *amico mio*. Where's Giovanna?" Tony took a whiskey from the tray the waiter held out. "Is that your secretary? She looks *hot* tonight. Why is she here? Taking minutes? Earning a little extra cash?"

"Hands off. She's with me. Sara is a damn good assistant. I have no intention of losing her." The jealousy that boiled in his gut at Tony's interest wasn't an emotion he was familiar with.

Tony let out a low whistle. "Easy, man. It's not like you to be so territorial."

"I'm protecting my business interests. I'd prefer it if you stayed away from her and don't try to get to know her better."

Tony grinned, a cheeky smile that had women the world over flat on their backs in seconds as soon as he was invited to. "Tell that to JT Horne. Your fancy Boston lawyer is putting his smooth moves on her right now."

"Like dogs on heat, the lot of you." Carmelo shoved his glass into Tony's hand. "Excuse me."

Tony laughed. "You were too once, but it looks like someone might be holding your balls hostage tonight!"

He ignored the jibe and bit down on a growl of

irritation as he crossed the deck to where JT had Sara cornered. "JT, my man, how was your cruise around the Whitsundays?" Carmelo delivered a friendly slap to his lawyer's shoulder, catching the look on Sara's face — fear mixed with apprehension. What could JT have done or said for her to be afraid? He was a big flirt, but he wouldn't harm a fly and never a woman. He liked them too much. "I see you've met my date."

"Your *date*? Where's —?" JT caught his warning look and changed tack. "Ah … okay. I was just saying there's something familiar about Sara. I can't quite think where I've seen her before."

"Around the office." He edged between them and put his hand on her arm. A flash of relief crossed her features. Carmelo frowned. Most women were flattered by JT's attention, impressed by his golden-boy good looks, Boston upbringing, and old money. Not Sara.

She wriggled out of his hold and stepped away. "If you would excuse me, please? I need to find the powder room."

"I'll show you the way," Carmelo offered, but she waved him off.

"No, stay and play host to your guests. If I get lost, I'll ask one of the crew for directions."

He studied her shapely legs carrying her away and wondered at her haste.

JT sipped his drink before saying, "You've lowered

your standards to the office help now? You're courting a sexual harassment suit if you have."

Anger — quick and territorial — flashed through him. "My reputation with women may earn that kind of slur, JT, but Sara doesn't deserve it."

"Man, you know I don't mean to offend you — or her — but she's way off the usual caliber of woman you have on your arm. I hope you know what you're doing."

"Right now, I'm not doing anything. Sara is helping me out tonight, that's all. It's all above board, complete with paid overtime." The sway of her hips as she made her way through the throng of guests towards the cabin had him thinking of all the things he'd like to do with Sara. None of which could become a reality if he wanted to keep his sanity.

"You keep telling yourself that. Right now, your eyes are telling a different story. You want a piece of that ass and paying her for it takes this little rendezvous to a whole new level of compensation payout."

"If you don't want my fist in your mouth, you're better off telling me what your plan is to bury this damn racing scandal once and for all." Sara disappeared from sight. His feet itched to follow her below deck. When had he lost his senses? He turned back to JT. "The press is hounding us over the Daytona Beach mess. They still think we're trying to cover our asses by blaming the disqualification on Meira and de la Cruz."

JT shrugged. "And good luck to them finding the

truth in that. We know that's not how it went down. They'll lose interest soon enough with only a few more races to go this season. Have they found her yet?"

Carmelo shook his head. Isadora de la Cruz had disappeared from the scene soon after bringing shame to his team. "She almost cost me everything I've worked hard for." Including the passion that had lifted him from the gutter to the top floor suite of one of San Francisco's most prestigious office precincts. "She's also left me without a team driver while she's most likely living it up with Meira on their blood money in Cancun. And I'm here a quarter of a million dollars in penalties lighter in the pocket, left to deal with the fallout."

"Being accused of race cheating isn't something you'll bounce back from easily. Once the trust is broken, the officials will scrutinize every part you change and every tweak you make to the motor or body. You're lucky they're allowing your team to race at all with only a two-race suspension."

"You think I don't know this, JT?" What was it with the women in his life that they were all so determined to strip him of his wealth one way or another? Isadora de la Cruz had screwed him without even making it into his bed. He hadn't even met the woman and she'd cost him a small fortune. His mistake. He shouldn't have trusted Meira's insistence that he could run the team solo.

"She'll show up. The smell of rubber, oil and money will bring her back to the track soon enough. It always does." JT slapped Carmelo's shoulder. "We'll be waiting for them when they resurface. I'm working on building a case. The Whitsundays wasn't all about lazing around in the sun and drinking cocktails on the beach."

Carmelo shrugged. He didn't want to think about Isadora de la Cruz right now. The taint of that name on his lips would erase the sweet taste of Sara Stewart and he wanted to savor that flavor a little while longer.

Chapter Five

Of all the people to be aboard the yacht tonight, one had to be JT Horne.

Isadora cursed as she clamped a fist to her stomach and took deep breaths to steady her heart rate. Although she'd only briefly met him once in the pits, he co-owned the race team with Carmelo. The game had just changed with the risk of recognition higher.

She'd had her race helmet on when he'd introduced himself, but JT was an observant man, and he had a copy of her race portfolio. A few added pounds, a ton of cosmetic disguise and a fake persona wouldn't fool a man like JT Horne for long, not when he'd invested hundreds of thousands of his own dollars into the team.

It might be small change for old Boston money, but the scandal would have tainted his reputation as a lawyer. The press maintained he'd known about the illegal suspension modifications and his hightailing it out to sea had only added fuel to the rumors.

Isadora found her way deep into the luxurious yacht, the furthest she could go. She'd heard about it — three decks above and two below the main deck — even seen photos, but never had she envisioned the sheer beauty of Carmelo's home away from home on the water.

Stately black and chrome staircases rose between decks, the décor either side modern with clean lines. Her heels clicked against Italian marble tiles in cream with threads of brown and black. A top interior designer had been commissioned to the yacht, and since she'd signed off on the purchase order, Isadora knew that only the best leather and wood had gone into furnishing it.

She reached a stateroom — Carmelo's. The scent of his cologne lingered in the air. Thick cream pile carpet soothed her feet as she removed her shoes. She curled her toes into the softness as she took in the interior.

Walnut finishes lent warmth to the room, bathed in golden light from the overhead crystal chandelier. Isadora's gaze skimmed over the king size bed with its plump pillows and semi turned down linen, ready for Carmelo to spend the night there.

Pushing open the door to the powder room, she leaned her head against the cool marble tiles on the wall, willing her mind to stop whirling and come up with an escape plan.

Out in the middle of the bay with the crowd on the party deck, slipping away unnoticed would be almost impossible. The motorboats that had brought them out to the yacht had returned to the dock. If the gossip rags were right, the party would go on all night, so they'd only be needed again in the morning.

All night parties and the resulting reports the following day led her to thinking about the more carnal edge that had become synonymous with Carmelo's social events.

With Giovanna out of the way, would Carmelo pair up with one of the long-legged beauties on deck? Not that it was any of her business except that she might need to find another place to hide if he did. Being stuck in his bathroom while he participated in wild party sex on that inviting bed wasn't exactly an attractive option.

Her thoughts turned sensual at the image that created. It didn't take much imagination to visualize him naked and aroused, spread out on that luxurious king-sized bed. Would he be a slow, steady lover or one driven by fast-paced passion?

Isadora closed her eyes to indulge in thoughts of how he'd looked standing at the rail earlier, framed against the view of the bay, with his shirt flapping loose in the breeze.

Would his abs be as washboard tight as they looked? Would his skin be warm and smooth under her hands? Desire – hot and strong — curled through her as she remembered the feel of his body against hers. Even through the barrier of clothing, she'd experienced a shot of need to be curled into him until they were touching … skin on skin.

Had she imagined the stir in his length against her? There'd be no doubt that Carmelo would be a very satisfying lover. Isadora clenched her thighs against the pool of need that made her body pulse. She pressed a hand against the ache to still it. No good could come from daydreaming.

"Sara?" Carmelo's voice filtered through the cabin. "Are you in here?"

Opening her eyes, she groaned at the intrusion. "Yes, just finishing up in here." Isadora stepped over to the basin. Turning on the faucet, she dipped her fingers under the cool stream and dabbed them to her cheeks.

"Everything okay?" This time the question came from outside the powder room door where it stood ajar.

"Yeah, all good." Isadora pressed a hand towel to her face, dabbing at the dampness, then folded and placed it on the counter. She turned to open the door and found him leaning against the frame.

He reached out to touch her cheek with a gentle finger. "I'm sorry. JT can be a bit overbearing."

"I should go. You don't need me here. These are your friends." She should move away, out of reach of the hand that now moved to cup her face. Instead the urge to lean into his touch grew harder to resist.

"Stay, please," he whispered, his thumb stroking across her cheekbone.

The noise of the party in full swing faded as her lips parted in protest. The warmth of his hand cupped her neck, drawing her closer. His mouth parted on a sigh before his head descended. The hunger in his kiss burned with a desperation that rose from deep within.

Isadora's nails curled into the bare skin of his chest, before spreading out her fingers for maximum contact. He whispered against her lips, but her mind refused to interpret the words as his arm slipped around her waist, drawing her into him.

Isadora burrowed into him; the hardness of his body pressed against her. All rational thought fled as his hands caressed her back, tightening on her curves to hold her hard against him, his mouth hungry.

Carmelo leaned back against the wall to take her weight, hitched her legs up around his waist and stroked the skin on her thigh, his fingers teasing at the lacy edge of her underwear. Joe's warning became a distant memory as the sensations his hands conjured had Isadora straining against him, hungry to feel him against the part of her that wanted him most.

His shirt fell from his shoulders under her hands exploring the solid muscles in his arms. Tearing her mouth from his, she nipped at the skin of his neck, traced her tongue along his collarbone. Need flared, a hungry fire that released her from her shy fake persona, allowed her to forget Sara Stewart and channel Isadora de la Cruz, the girl with red hot blood in her veins.

Carmelo's hands found that sweet spot, his fingers stroking the warm folds through silk and lace as he pushed away from the wall. Alarm bells rang in Isadora's mind. If she didn't stop it now, there'd be no going back. No forgiveness. No retribution. His fingers stroked and caressed, his head found the pillow of her breasts, and Isadora lost herself in a sea of sensation.

Her back hit the soft mattress and the magic of his hands disappeared. She barely had time to breathe before he hesitated over her, studied every inch of her, his doubts and desires a flash of expressions racing across his features.

"Sara?"

This was it. Her cue to tell him no, to stop this madness before she had to face him in the office on Monday morning. He stood, tall and straight beside the bed, his shirt slipping to floor along with any thought of rejection. The only regret she'd have would be if she couldn't have him tonight.

Isadora sat up to reach for the button of his trousers, loosened it, drew down his zipper and pushed the material down over his hips. His trousers fell to the floor and he kicked them aside.

A harsh cry ripped from his throat as her mouth touched the skin that pulled taut across his abdomen, her tongue tasting the textures and rippling muscles, finding the grooves, and caressing them. His hands released the tie of her halter neck dress and drew down the zipper. It fell away between them, releasing breasts that ached for his touch.

Isadora took her time to lick and kiss her way up the length of his torso, his hands finding the weight of her breasts, the pebbled nipples. She moaned against him as his fingers tugged and rolled. Then his hands were on her face, drawing her up his body, gently pushing her back onto the mattress before possessing her mouth with his.

She lifted her hips as he eased her dress down and tossed it onto the floor. Silk and lace followed until they were where they wanted to be — skin on skin.

With barely an inch between them, Carmelo traced the shape of her face with a tender touch, his eyes full of promises. "Last chance to tell me to stop."

"Please don't stop."

A smile, soft and sweet, touched his mouth. He reached over Isadora's head to the drawer that would hold the only barrier between them tonight.

Isadora took the foil packet from him, opened it, and sheathed his length. "No regrets," she whispered, holding his gaze.

Whatever happened in the morning, they had this one night. One night where he could take away the ache of being a shadow of her true self, and the farce of pretending to be someone she wasn't. No regrets, no revenge, only release.

Every bit as beautiful as she'd expected him to be, he balanced himself over her on strong arms. From the bronze of his skin to the taut muscles of his very touch-worthy ass, her hands tingled to touch every inch of him and to feel that heat under her fingertips.

His hands stroked; tripping nerve ends into tiny shocks that shuddered through her. The hot graze of his lips found her body, sensations searing every inch of her skin.

Isadora wrapped her hand around his length, drew him down, shuddered with pleasure as his hardness slipped inside her. She held his gaze; every slow, measured stroke of his touch filling her with ecstasy until he thrust home with a cry she echoed and he kissed her mind into oblivion.

Spent, she lay in his arms, her head on his chest and his heartbeat in her ear. Reality rushed in. What had she done? Isadora squeezed her eyes shut and held her breath on a whimper as disgust gate-crashed her euphoria.

She'd had sex with the man who'd stripped her pride, stolen her life and destroyed her dreams. And she was halfway to being in love with him.

Chapter Six

I sadora stretched out the kinks in her muscles with the languorous satisfaction of a woman well-loved. She wanted to enjoy this moment a little longer before good sense came knocking on the door.

Carmelo had gone, but his scent and the indent of his head on the pillow remained, a reminder of what they'd shared. No man had ever made her feel quite so special as he'd kissed every inch of her skin, worshipped every curve and dip of her body.

As the haze of sleep and satisfaction cleared from her mind, the throb of the twin engines registered. A gentle roll to the right had her sitting up in bed. The yacht was on the move. The digital clock on the table next to Isadora blinked the time in red numerals — 9.30 a.m. What the hell? He hadn't mentioned anything about leaving the Bay. She had a cat to feed. Luckily, she'd had the foresight to put out some pellets for Cruzer before leaving home last night.

Isadora threw the covers aside, groaned at her nakedness and searched for her clothes. Gone. Who on earth would take her clothes?

A tap at the door and a tentative, "Excuse me, Miss Stewart?" had her scurrying back between the sheets and pulling them up to her neck.

"Come in, please."

The door opened and a maid came in carrying a breakfast tray. The smell of eggs and bacon and something sweet raised a growl from her stomach reminding her that she hadn't eaten the night before.

"Good morning, Miss Stewart. My name is Maria. Please ask me for anything you need. Mr Iannello says to meet him on deck when you've finished your breakfast."

And how the hell would she do that naked? The crew of the *Bay Princess* had seen a lot of things that would scandalize most, but Isadora had no intention of adding to the portfolio of Carmelo's mistresses they may have seen naked.

The maid smiled knowingly but not unkindly as she laid the tray across Isadora's knees and fluffed out the pillows behind her back. How many women had she had to do that for in the past? The full force of last night's actions rolled over her like a category five cyclone. She'd succeeded in seducing the great Carmelo Iannello.

She'd wanted to bring him to his knees and she had, with spectacular results that could hardly be considered punishment.

Had she been to bed with the playboy or the man? Did it matter? If she was into emotional blackmail, she'd have the perfect case against him to destroy his reputation. He too had slept with the enemy. She could twist that to her advantage in so many ways ... except she no longer wanted to.

If she'd seen the real Carmelo last night, her plans for revenge were in trouble. There was no way in hell the man who'd paid such loving homage to her body was capable of the things she'd suspected of him — lying, cheating, and gambling with his employees' futures. Neither the honesty in his eyes nor the soft whispers against her skin added up to a man who would ruthlessly destroy someone's world as he had hers.

"I've laundered your evening clothes, Miss Stewart. Fresh clothes suited to sailing in the bay will be arriving for you shortly."

Mortification slammed into her, giving rise to a blush that stemmed from her toes up. *Oh dear God*. The ease with which the maid set about her tasks proved how many times she'd done this before. Isadora was just one woman in a long line of bed partners. She wanted to ask how on earth Maria had managed to secure the right dress size but with practice came experience.

"Thank you, Maria."

If the guests had already gone home, she and Carmelo would be alone and that could be dangerous. The time had come to extract herself from the mess she'd created by falling into bed with the boss. Quitting her job wasn't an option until she'd regained her good reputation and bedding the enemy wasn't the best way to go about clearing her name.

"You're welcome. Will that be all, Miss Stewart?"

"Yes, thank you." Heat flared in Isadora's cheeks. Dare she ask for clean underwear and toiletries? The remnants of last night's scattered silk and lace were nowhere to be seen.

Perhaps it was the burn that scorched her face that gave away her thoughts. Or maybe Maria herself had removed the torn remnants of her favorite red thong from the floor which would be most embarrassing. The maid smiled kindly, a twinkle of amusement in her dark eyes.

"Whatever you need, I have arranged." She turned and left the cabin, pulling the door closed behind her.

Shame shoved embarrassment out of the way in a race to churn in Isadora's stomach. What had she become? She set the tray aside and pushed back the covers. To the right the powder room beckoned. The mirror above the elegant wash basin revealed the remains of last night's makeup and red welts on her neck that looked awfully like ... *Oh good grief!* Love bites?

Anger rose from her belly and thoughts of revenge

resurfaced. He had no right to leave evidence of what had passed between them. But wasn't that true of Carmelo Iannello's style? To brand his mistresses? And now she was one of them. To hell with him! She'd go right up on deck and confront him, expose her true self, and take back what was left of her pride ... as soon as Maria brought her some clothes.

Carmelo turned his back on the doorway leading to the lower deck. Watching for her would only alert JT to how differently he felt about Sara. The dark looks he threw Carmelo's way clearly spoke of his distaste. It wouldn't be long before he voiced his opinion. They knew each other too well for JT not to see the change.

"You're distracted."

JT's voice reached him where he clutched the cold aluminum rail that ran the length of the portside stern. Carmelo turned his head to watch the foam of the wake spread out into the waters of the Bay. They were headed for Angel Island and his skipper was taking his own sweet time about it. As ordered. An uneasiness settled in his stomach — that feeling that something was about to happen and it wouldn't be good.

"A little." Carmelo shrugged off the churn impatiently. "I'm tired, JT. This Florida race scandal has not only eaten away at my pocket, but it's also stolen my passion. Now the press will be pounding on my door over dumping Giovanna and the race wear deal. When did I drop the ball on my life?"

"Who says you've dropped the ball?"

"The whole mess has me questioning my goals. Have I come this far, achieved this much only to have it destroyed by a cheating, lying woman who cost the team the race? How much did she take in bribes to make it worth her while to lose the race that would have made her a champion?"

JT strolled up. Turning his back to the rail, foot casually placed on the lower bar and his palms resting on the top, he eyed Carmelo thoughtfully for a moment. "Is it the woman or the scandal bothering you?"

"Neither. I paid my debt to the tribunal for that race. The money means nothing. It's the betrayal that irks me still."

"This wasn't your doing. Those suspension changes she ordered were illegal. She'd have known that."

Carmelo tilted his head to look up as the yacht sailed under the giant red structure of Golden Gate Bridge. "She'll never race again. That's penance enough for any driver. The track has its own form of justice." He didn't want to talk about this, not while discontent rattled inside him. "Beats me as to why a driver with such an impeccable record would throw a race like that knowing it could destroy their career."

Ice seeped into JT's tone. "There is only one reason.

Money. Big money. And she had a large amount of it down on a bet to win according to investigations by the race officials. She fixed the race for financial gain."

"Isadora de la Cruz came to my team a number one driver. Until the scandal, she was highly respected in the racing community. Her first race on my team and she screwed me over. Perhaps if I'd had the chance to meet her personally before that race, I wouldn't feel so betrayed by her deception. I should have interviewed her myself. Or perhaps I should have looked more closely at her boyfriend before I gave him the job as team manager."

JT shrugged. "He too came with impeccable references. Enough for you to trust him to handle that race in your absence."

"A move I now regret deeply. Their deception almost lost me everything. My business is still feeling the aftershocks. If people don't believe in me, if they think I'm a liar and a cheat, how can I expect them to believe in my product?"

"No one saw that race disqualification coming. Not even me. And I drew up their contracts. No one suspected Meira and de la Cruz were in cahoots. Their affair and the race debacle aside, she is — was — a damn savvy driver, and he had a good reputation as a team manager. There was nothing in either of their backgrounds to indicate any questionable behavior."

"Yeah, well maybe we should have looked a little

harder." Carmelo shoved his hands into the pockets of his cargo shorts.

"Isadora de la Cruz came from well-respected racing blood. Her father was one of the most iconic drivers in NASCAR history. The straightest arrow you could find. As for Harlon Meira, he came with good references. I trusted him as much as you did, but he was smart at keeping secrets. We will earn public trust again, Carmelo. We just need to be smart about it."

"That's why I called off the launch of the race wear. I need to make sure it's a product an investor can trust. I can't afford another loss." Not when he'd worked so hard to put money in the bank. He never wanted to taste the bitter sting of starvation and homelessness again. While the probability of that was slim, he still didn't like throwing away good money on poor investments.

"We both lost that race, my friend. It's a hard lesson we've learned, but we need to move on."

"To what? I see nothing in the future. No challenge." Carmelo threw open his hands to the Bay. "I'm tired of being a plaything for society, JT. The women, the parties, the wealth … it all feels meaningless now."

JT chuckled. "Maybe we're growing up, evolving. My mother would agree it's time."

Carmelo sighed. "This playboy image that follows me around is fast losing its attraction. There is this … void inside me. I go home at night to a house that echoes with emptiness and I'm reminded of the home I grew up in filled with love, warmth, and laughter, until that too was stolen from me. There is something missing from my life and I need to find it. Press the reset button and start over."

"You can start over by finishing whatever it was you engaged in with your personal assistant last night. That's dangerous territory, even for a risk-taker like you. She's not the right girl for you."

"Damn it, JT, for a few hours last night it felt like she could be, but in reality, I took advantage of her vulnerability last night. Another mistake on my growing rap sheet."

Warm, cuddly Sara with her blonde hair, sweet curves and satin skin, and a deep-seated passion she'd unleashed in him over and over again last night. A girl the total opposite of lying, cheating Isadora de la Cruz whose portfolio photograph portrayed a svelte, dark-haired go-getter with a thirst for pole position and money.

He turned to face the same direction as JT to watch the Golden Gate Bridge recede on the horizon. His gaze fell on the doorway and there she was. Blonde hair ruffled by the breeze, a navy blue and white scarf knotted at her neck to cover the branding of their shared passion. God knew he bore a few marks from it too.

Maria had done well picking out clothes for Sara. She'd captured the essence of the vintage look Sara favored. Capri pants caressed her curves like his hands had last night and wanted to again this morning. A white crop top stretched across breasts that fitted his palms perfectly. And in the gap in between, the skin he'd kissed every inch of beckoned to him once more.

"I will finish it." A promise that made regret burn in his gut, because with Sara he'd experienced peace and satisfaction in a way he hadn't for a long time. He'd slept deeply with her at his side last night when previously sleep had evaded him for months. And when she was awake, with her hands touching his skin, he felt alive.

Chapter Seven

Thoughts of revenge fled as Isadora caught sight of Carmelo at the rail with JT. Nerves rattled her heart and the burning sensation of guilt threatened the resurgence of breakfast. Apprehension churned through her. Had JT worked out who she was? In daylight without the shadows to hide in, she'd be a lot easier to identify.

JT Horne was smart enough to see through a disguise no matter how different she looked masquerading as Sara Stewart. Carmelo could too, except he was used to seeing her every day and he'd never met Isadora de la Cruz. Or perhaps all he saw was the body he'd feasted on with a hungry need that stemmed from somewhere deep inside of him.

He'd never looked too closely at her, not even last night. He'd kept his eyes closed every time, as if he didn't need sight because the sensations of touching alone were good enough. And they had been. Each caress, or sweep of his mouth, had turned her bones to jelly. Her skin had tingled at the touch of his fingertips. And when he'd filled her, she'd felt complete. Whole. The only time he'd opened his eyes was at the peak of passion when he'd looked so deep into hers, he could easily have seen her soul and the guilt that squeezed at her heart.

No. Isadora wouldn't be swayed by sex so good it blew her mind and made her believe in happy ever after. She couldn't afford to. If she did, her reputation, her career, her life would remain in tatters and Carmelo would have won. She had to get back on track. Digging deep, she dredged up the anger born out of humiliation.

The rubber soles of her sailing shoes squeaked against the wooden deck as she made her way over to the two men. JT settled back against the rail, arms folded across his chest, eyes narrowed as he studied her, his gaze intense. Like an X-ray she feared would see right through her facade.

The frown on Carmelo's face vanished, replaced by a warm smile that made her heart jump. His eyes scanned Isadora's body and heat spread up from her core. She closed her thoughts to the wave of desire that crashed through her. She'd need a sharp mind in the presence of JT Horne and Carmelo's heated gaze melted her good sense.

Needing the splash of ice water, she greeted JT first.

His eyes narrowed on hers, icy blue. "Good morning, Sara. I trust you slept well?"

She held his gaze only long enough to offer a polite response before she turned to Carmelo, carefully keeping her hands locked behind her back, the temptation to touch him too great. "You never said anything about leaving the Bay." She wanted to be angry with him for breaking his promise but how could she be with him staring at her with an intensity that made her want to kiss him again.

"A day trip." Smooth velvet tones enveloped her, warming the chill that had nothing to do with the wind off the Bay and everything to do with guilt and self-disgust. "We're going to picnic on Angel Island before returning for dinner at Indovinare in Sausalito."

Indovinare. The most sought-after restaurant in San Francisco. Society paid a fortune just to secure a table there and the waiting list was months long. Isadora felt every bit the fraud she'd become.

"Great. I'll catch a cab home from Sausalito and leave you to it."

Carmelo stepped closer, his hands warm on her cold arms, his body aligned with hers. She only had to take a small step forward to be in his arms, against him, absorbing his heat.

"Stay. Please."

Only a saint could ignore the plea in his eyes. And

Isadora was no saint. The length of his forefinger brushed her cheek and tucked a lock of hair behind her ear. His eyes followed the movement before he pressed a kiss to her forehead. An involuntary sigh escaped Isadora's lips. Perhaps she could pretend this was real for a little while longer. A dangerous gamble.

"What more do you want from me, Carmelo? The party is over."

"I'd like you to stay, spend the day with me." His palm cupped her face, lifting it to his.

Was she strong enough to take what was on offer and suffer the consequences later? She would use what he'd done to her career against him, but she couldn't use what had happened between them last night as a weapon. Not this warm, tender touch, nor the passion that consumed him even now as his mouth descended on hers.

JT Horne, *Fit to Race*, Isadora's goals as a NASCAR driver — none of it mattered, not right now. Not when his lips were sweet with the taste of breakfast champagne and his tongue teased hers, drawing a whimper from somewhere deep inside her.

Isadora curled her fists into his shirt as she met each demand and issued a few of her own on his mouth, her legs weakening. Her mind swam with delicious sensations and all she wanted was to lose herself in his essence, in this moment.

The hand on her back, fingers spread, urged her

closer until every inch of their bodies lined up and every ragged breath he drew danced with hers. It wasn't possible that a man as cold and calculated as she'd believed Carmelo to be could put so much heart into a kiss. Is this what it felt like to be truly loved?

Ice crept up Isadora's spine. What on earth was she thinking? She dragged her mouth from his and stepped back. Over Carmelo's shoulder, JT's smirk taunted her, his mocking eyebrow raised. He shook his head and walked away, shattering the magic of the moment, making her feel every bit the lying, cheap, dirty lay he thought she was.

Why should she care? JT Horne meant nothing to her and neither did Carmelo. This was a means to an end. The payback for what they'd done to her career. A bittersweet victory, the perks of which she was entitled to enjoy. Except victory had a hollow ring to it when her own heart was at stake.

Carmelo's hands cupped her face. "Where did you go?"

The tight smile she forced to her lips hurt, but her heart hurt even more at the angry look in his eyes as she said, "I don't like to perform for an audience."

Carmelo stepped away and turned around to face the Bay, raking a hand through his hair. "You think I'm putting on a show. You're wrong. You know, for the first time ever, I feel I don't need to. Not with you. You make me comfortable. I'm not sure what to do about that. I've never felt that way before."

Isadora shrugged. His words made her stomach flip with joy, but she couldn't let herself believe that what they had going on between them had a future. "What happened last night—"

"Was no mistake."

"No, but your reputation demands it. Your friends expect it. I don't work that way. I'm not cut out to be one of your never-ending line of girlfriends. Someone you go to in your little black book of contacts when you need an escort. Last night *was* a mistake – mine, not yours." If she didn't dredge up her anger now, it would be lost and she'd become a slave to Carmelo's whim because – God help her – it would be so easy to do. "I shouldn't have let it happen."

Carmelo laughed, the sound harsh, mocking. "I didn't hear you complaining last night."

Isadora grimaced. "Your reputation lives up to the rumors, no doubt about that. One night, Carmelo, that's all I can give you. I need to keep my job." More than he'd ever know. She couldn't afford to be distracted by him when proving her innocence was paramount to continuing her career in NASCAR and he was the one responsible for ending it. "I can't do that if we continue this ... whatever it is we have."

He shoved his hands into the hip pockets of his cargo shorts, his head hanging low. "Your job is safe."

Then he turned to her and lifted his face, the full force of his gaze slamming into hers, rocketing to the pit of her stomach. "If you spend the weekend with me."

Distaste stung on her tongue. "That's blackmail and appalling."

A shadow crossed his features. "That's how much I need you."

If she lost this job, she wouldn't have open access to the information she needed to prove her innocence. All the work she'd done in the last few months — compiling repair records, tracing back parts orders, investigating suppliers who might have sold Harlon the illegal suspension parts and trying to tie it all back to Carmelo's instructions to perform the modifications — all of it would be for nothing.

Equally, by agreeing to his ultimatum and spending another night in his bed, she'd be digging herself deeper into a hole instead of out of it.

Chapter Eight

Already he missed having her in his arms, his hunger for her so great he didn't care who was watching.

JT's warning niggled at the edge of Carmelo's thoughts. Sara wasn't the girl for him. JT had that right. But for now, he harbored a deep-seated need to ease the ache of emptiness inside him. Even if only for a little while.

Somewhere in the hours before dawn, watching Sara sleep, he'd realized that he'd only ever loved a woman for her body, never her heart. Perhaps he was afraid that if he did, he'd love only one woman for the rest of his life ... one who would destroy him. Women like Giovanna who only saw what they could take and never gave anything back.

Unlike Sara who, since he'd tasted her, appeared to have spoiled his taste for another. He hated how vulnerable that made him. And so he'd resorted to blackmail. It gave him back control, power — a heady combination that had the old Carmelo rearing his head.

"Come on, Sara. Friends with benefits. This weekend only. And you get to keep your job on Monday."

"You ... asshole!"

He waited for the slap, would welcome it when it came. He deserved the punishment heading his way as the insult found its target. But the retaliation didn't come. Instead tears welled in her green eyes, turning them emerald in the sunlight and he felt every inch the asshole she'd called him.

Fire lit her eyes, her mouth set in a determined line as she advanced on him. God help him, he wanted to kiss that fire out of her. The sharp stab of her fingernail hit him square in the chest.

"You *absolute* asshole!"

Carmelo closed his fist around her hand, raised that accusing finger to his lips, nibbled at the pad and watched the fire in her eyes flare into something new.

Wrapping his arms around her, he gathered her close, caught her tears with his lips, the taste sweet and salty on his tongue. "But you knew that, Sara. Yet you still came to me."

Regret crept in at the stiffness of her body in his hold. Although he wasn't entirely sure which part he should regret the most. Hurting her? Yes. Sleeping with her? No. Using her for his own selfish needs? Definitely.

Cupping her head to his shoulder with one hand, he pressed her closer with the other. On the horizon, over her soft blonde crown, Angel Island loomed. Respite had come in whatever form it took and he welcomed the distance it would put between them. He'd been here a thousand times. Knew every inch of the place. Welcomed the familiar territory over the unfamiliar one he found himself in with Sara in his arms, feeling like she belonged there. As the engines geared back to drop anchor, she pulled out of his hold.

"I'll be leaving you at Sausalito. You can do what you please when Monday comes."

"Please stay. I'll put you in the cabin next to mine and I won't bother you again."

So he'd resorted to begging now. If Sara wasn't there, the weekend would stretch out before him like Groundhog Day. JT was great company but he didn't fill the emptiness inside him like this woman did.

She chewed her lip, the pearly white of her teeth stark against the red of her mouth. He ached for the graze of those teeth against his skin, prayed he'd feel that sensation one last time before reality intruded on their world.

"What happened last night can't happen again." Her words were barely audible over the engines, her lashes spiked damply against her cheeks as she squeezed her eyes shut, no doubt regretting her agreement to this madness.

"I'm not sure I can keep that promise." He let out a sigh. "But I will do my best to so that I'll have your company for at least one more day." He turned to rest his elbows on the aluminum rail and pretended to admire the view. "The beauty of Angel Island takes my breath away every time." Almost in the same way Sara had stolen his breath last night.

As the yacht sailed into the cove, the island loomed on the left. The narrow strip of sand gave way to a rising hill with dark green vegetation lush against the backdrop of blue water. A few smaller sailing boats had beaten them to it, their sails furled below bare masts. The hull of the *Bay Princess* was too deep for the reef, so the captain would dock at the mouth and they'd use the dinghy to reach the beach.

The sound of the anchor being dropped reached his ears around the same time as JT's voice and the answering giggle of his weekend companion. A week ago, he'd been just like his lawyer friend.

On Sunday night, JT would wave his girlfriend goodbye with the promise of a phone call and never see her again. Carmelo would have to face Sara across his desk on Monday knowing every inch of her skin under her clothes and have to treat her like just another employee once more. Something she'd never be again.

The electric grind of the winch lowering the dinghy into the water interrupted his thoughts and he turned to reach for Sara's hand. "I'll help you down."

She hesitated, her mouth determined, her eyes reflecting the doubt in her mind. "I don't need your help."

"Why don't we call a truce? Just for today. It's a beautiful day. The sun is out, the birds are singing and the world is an amazing place." Carmelo smiled and beckoned for her to come closer. "Come along. Think of it as a reward of a day out for all the work you've done." As her hand filled his palm — warm and soft — a snap of desire coursed through him, catching him unaware. He wished they were alone so he could exorcise her from his mind, but that might be harder to do than any other challenge he'd faced in his thirty-two years.

Her body brushed against his as he drew her closer, enclosed her waist with his arm. He pressed a reassuring kiss to her temple but it made him want to kiss her mouth instead. His body grew hard and his need even greater. Sara had bewitched him, body, and soul.

Carmelo held her a moment longer, her beautiful eyes on his. The flicker in them telling him all he needed to know. Despite her resistance and anger, she wasn't immune.

He let her go, tugged her towards the ladder to the swim platform where the wooden dinghy waited — his pride and joy. Carmelo and JT had crafted it themselves the summer *Fit to Race* was born, when JT had become an investor, his lawyer and a good friend, the only person willing to take a chance on a man who had once been a kid off the streets.

Carmelo had to release Sara's hand to start the engine and take control of the tiller. She sat close, her thigh rubbing against his on the slotted wood of the seat as the dinghy dipped to the play of the waves.

He let his gaze rest on her face, her expression of wonder, as she tilted her head to take in the spectacular view that was Angel Island. She'd swept her hair back into a ponytail. The tilt of her chin, the creamy curve of her neck and the essence of Sara had his heart picking up speed along with his desire for her.

It was then he noticed the small tattoo of a white dove perched on top of a red helmet on the skin behind her ear. Carmelo frowned. He'd seen that tattoo somewhere before. Reaching out he traced the pattern with his finger.

Sara whipped her head away, her hand flying up to cover the tattoo, her eyes slamming into his before darting away again. She pulled the elastic band out of her hair and it fell in waves around her shoulders, covering the artwork.

"What does it mean?" Her reaction intrigued him.

She'd been so quick to hide it, her hands trembling as she'd loosened her hair.

"It's nothing. Just a silly tattoo I had done a long time ago."

It might be nothing, but it had upset her that he'd seen it. That churning feeling of foreboding resurfaced in Carmelo's gut. He pushed it away. A girl like Sara would have nothing to hide, no reason to lie. She wasn't like those who mixed in his circles, not worldly-wise or manipulative. She appeared too innocent for that.

In the bow with his arm around his companion, Carmelo caught JT studying Sara intently. A short, sharp stab of jealousy replaced the unease and took him by surprise. Not once had he ever cared whether JT eyed out his dates. This was the first time he'd cared enough about one to notice.

Ignoring the jab, he let the hand that wasn't on the tiller rest possessively on Sara's thigh and changed the subject. "It's hard to believe the island was almost razed by fire in '08. Took out almost two hundred and fifty acres."

"It's beautiful now," she said, her tone tainted by a nervousness he didn't understand, her hand worrying the waves of blonde that covered her ear and hid the tattoo.

JT's gaze narrowed as he withdrew his arm and leaned forward, elbows on his knees, arms folded, features deceptively innocent. Carmelo knew that look well. It was the one he used just before going in for the kill in a court case. One that sealed a deal or tossed it out the door. Doubt returned to Carmelo's mind, stirring the contents of his stomach into heartburn. JT was onto something and he didn't like it. His friend's gut instinct had seldom proved wrong in the past.

"I didn't picture you as the type to get inked, Sara." JT tapped his fingers on his forearm.

Sara shuffled on the seat and pulled at the crease in her capri pants. "Er ... no, I'm not. I ... this was something special."

"Special? How?"

Her shoulders stiffened and her spine snapped into alignment as she sat straighter on the seat. "Does it matter? I'm not sure it's any of your business."

Her lashes flickered, but she didn't back off. Instead she stared JT down and Carmelo's admiration for her grew. Not many people could make JT Horne uncomfortable. There was a lot more to Sara Stewart he didn't know yet.

"Back off, JT." Carmelo didn't try to disguise the growl in his command.

Even though he knew to trust his friend's instincts, JT's suspicions were an unwelcome intrusion. Any other weekend, he enjoyed sailing the Bay with the man who'd been his friend since JT had helped him get back on his feet. This weekend was different, though. For the first time in his life, he wanted to be alone with a woman for longer than a night.

Carmelo cut the engine and let the dinghy drift closer to the pier. Whatever it was JT thought he knew, it could wait.

Chapter Nine

Isadora's heart pounded as she avoided looking at Carmelo. He'd see her vulnerability. God damn JT Horne to hell. He was heavily invested in the racing scene, he'd seen her resume, and he knew who her father was. It wouldn't take him long to string the information together and for her to be exposed. She went with as much truth as she could.

"The tattoo is in memory of my father. He died from an intracranial hemorrhage sustained from a head trauma in a car accident."

She should thank JT for reminding her of the reason she was here. They'd accused her of cheating and had brought shame to the de la Cruz name. She'd make them pay. One way or another. And the taste of revenge would be sweet.

"That's enough now, JT. Come, Sara." Carmelo's

voice was gentle, apologetic, his hand extended palm up.

She placed her hand in his, felt the curl of his fingers around her. The dinghy swayed on the gentle waves in the cove, toppling her against him. For a moment, she absorbed his warmth then hated herself for needing it. In his embrace, she could forget who she was, set aside the ugliness of the world, and the shattered dreams that lay around her. But she could never forgive him for breaking her heart or stealing that race from her through greed. For ordering illegal modifications that would make the car two seconds faster and guarantee a win. For not trusting her to win the race on skill. She had to see this through.

He released his hold and climbed up onto the pier, all long legs and rippling muscle. It wasn't hard to understand what made women fall at his feet. His dark, bad boy sexiness was a drawcard for trouble. And to date his worst crime was his playboy reputation and the string of broken hearts he left in his wake. That and the destruction of her career.

He hoisted Isadora up alongside him, the muscles in his forearms bunching, his hands strong, fingers warm and firm around her wrists. Everywhere his skin grazed hers, tiny goosebumps of pleasure raised in the wake of his touch, echoed through her blood, and made it fizz with desire for him. This madness had to stop.

Then his fingers threaded through hers and he drew

her to his side as they walked the length of the pier towards the picnic tables scattered across the lawn above the beach. Her gaze took in the contrast of green against sandy-colored beach and the bright blue water beyond. Californian sunshine sparkled off the water against the backdrop of Point Tiburon.

Isadora lifted her face to the sun and let the warmth seep into her to ease the freeze in her heart. JT was like a dog worrying a bone. A bulldog that wouldn't let go until he'd stripped that bone bare of the flesh. She'd need her wits about her for the afternoon that stretched ahead.

They stopped at a table overlooking the pier and a view across Ayala Cove. Carmelo turned to her, one hand still on hers, the other a feather light touch of fingertips on her waist in the gap between her capri pants and top.

"JT and I will collect the picnic hamper from the cafe." He pressed his lips to her cheek, trailed a kiss to the skin beneath her ear.

Isadora shivered, closed her eyes, and leaned into him for that split second before he stepped away. The space he left filled with emptiness.

She smiled and turned to Aylesha who studied her manicure with interest and ignored the view. Her cheerleader good looks bore the imprint of Hollywood's fascination with fillers. Plumped up lips that barely moved when she smiled, a brow that remained frozen in an expressionless face. This was the kind of woman

Carmelo usually favored. Track groupies who craved the lifestyle racing money could buy.

Conversation was pointless. Isadora found it sad that girls like Aylesha closed their minds and allowed themselves to be used and tossed aside on a playboy's whim. Like a privilege they'd earned or a sacrifice they'd had to make to get what they wanted — lifestyle, status, and fame.

But who was she to judge? Hadn't she put herself in the same position for Carmelo this weekend? No amount of justification for her cause would make her any different. She'd fallen hard from the first kiss. Except, it had nothing to do with money and everything to do with pure, white-hot desire.

Isadora sat down at the picnic bench and tucked her hands under her thighs, palms flat against the wood. With the sun warm on her shoulders and the magic of the view before her, she let the peacefulness of Angel Island chase away the tension from her spine.

For just one day, she wanted to forget the race, the humiliation, the loss. She was here, in a tiny slice of paradise, with a man who did wicked things to her blood. Later she'd remind herself he was the enemy. Today she wanted to know the man, the lover. Revenge would still be there on Monday.

Laughter, deep and easy, reached her ears. She turned her head to see Carmelo and JT returning with the picnic hamper between them. This was the most relaxed she'd ever seen him. The usually firm set of Carmelo's mouth curved up in a smile, the tension lifted from his shoulders and the grooves normally carved into his cheeks by concentration deepened with humor not annoyance.

And she wanted him. For this weekend, the enjoyment of Carmelo Iannello's body belonged to her. She doubted anyone would ever own his heart. Isadora wasn't even sure he had one. Perhaps there was another layer to him? One he didn't show to the public.

No, she couldn't afford to think he might be human. If she did, she'd forget what he'd done to her, to her father's memory. She was thankful though that it seemed JT had let the awkward moment in the dinghy go. She'd dodged a bullet. For now.

Isadora stood as they approached, clearing the way for them to set the hamper down on the picnic table. Her heart fluttered as Carmelo's dark gaze captured hers. If eyes could speak, the message in his was clear. He was as into her as she was him. If they'd been alone ...

Giving herself a mental shake, she dropped her gaze to the basket and fiddled with the strap to release the lid. She pushed it up and let it drop over the back of the hamper. Lifting the tablecloth covering the food, she peeked inside. On a deep plate, plump pink shrimp rested on a bed of shaved ice. Fresh oysters cozied up on another plate. Juicy roast chicken with rich, golden, crispy skin decorated a platter lined with fresh green lettuce. A colorful garden salad drew Aylesha's attention from her nails but it was the bottle of Grand Vintage *Moet et Chandon* that held it.

A smile stretched Isadora's lips. Priorities. Not that she blamed her. A glass of ice-cold champagne would take the edge off the heat that grew inside her as Carmelo's fingers stroked her cheek and traced her smile.

He dropped his hand and flicked the tablecloth out over the surface. "Hungry, Sara?"

She shivered. Yes, but not for food. Isadora ignored Carmelo's question, JT's humorless laugh and the humiliation that simmered inside her to arrange the feast on the table. Carmelo moved to take the basket, his arm brushing against her.

Her hand shook a little on the bowl of plump, red strawberries, so she steadied it, not wanting to give JT any more reason to focus on her. The hamper seemed bottomless as she drew out olives, cheeses, crackers, and *pates*. Isadora arranged them all on the tablecloth and began removing the plastic wrap from the feast while Carmelo popped the cork on the champagne. JT held out the flutes, tipped carefully to avoid the fizz from overflowing down the crystal stems. Aylesha looked like all she needed was the bottle and a straw.

Perhaps she wasn't as comfortable in this environment as Isadora had first thought. Aylesha eyed the shrimp and oysters in horror, her pale skin taking on a green tinge. Taking pity on her, Isadora offered her the bowl of salad and a plate.

"Would you like chicken with that?"

The haughtiness of earlier returned as Aylesha dropped her designer sunglasses over her eyes. "No."

Isadora smiled. She was used to the haughtiness of models. Every racetrack in the world attracted them like bees to honey. The ice in her tone didn't bother Isadora, but the look of hatred that flashed in the girl's eyes did. A shiver ran through her. She couldn't afford to make an enemy out of JT's girlfriend.

Beside her Carmelo chuckled, his arm slipping around her waist, his palm caressing the curve of her hip. He picked up a shrimp by the tail and held it to her lips. Isadora opened her mouth and allowed the flavor of fresh San Francisco flesh to kiss her tongue. With a sigh of appreciation, she nipped down and left the tail between Carmelo's fingers. "Oh ... God, that's good."

Heat flared in his eyes as he held up another, waiting patiently for her to finish chewing. His hand on her hip urged her closer into the hardness of his body. There was no mistaking the effect of her sounds of satisfaction were having on him.

She'd never had that much power over a man and it was heady, unleashing a hungry beast inside her.

This time, she touched her tongue to his fingertips, holding his stare as she did so. His eyes widened, the pupils dilating against a bed of rich, dark brown, his gaze darkening with desire. Her teeth grazed his skin as she bit off the tail.

Isadora had barely swallowed before his mouth devoured the final flavors of the shrimp on her tongue. His arms enveloped her, drawing her squarely against his desire. She whimpered with the need to feel him; hot, hard, and aroused.

Around her, Angel Island faded to a haze. His hands worked magic on her back, blazing a trail up her spine until they cupped her cheeks and his tongue delved deeper to tease hers. Then all she could taste was Carmelo. The tart bite of *Moet* mixed with desire, and the essence of man.

The stubble on his chin grazed her skin and she lifted her hands to his face, caressed the day-old growth of beard on his jaw, closed her eyes to savor the feel of it against her palms. In the back of her mind a warning bell rang. She was caught in a rip tide and drowning.

Chapter Ten

Carmelo drew back far enough to whisper, "If it is possible to get drunk on the taste of a woman, then I am beyond redemption." Even the feel of her soft hands against his face drove him insane with need. Only the ice in JT's voice cooled the passion that roared within.

"Knock it off, Carmelo. This is a family-friendly island."

Irritation skimmed his nerve ends, and not for the first time this weekend he wished JT had gone ashore after the party. And what was his problem with Sara? Sure, he was playing with fire here, but that wasn't what worried him. It wasn't only lust driving this need within him. That alone should have him bundling Sara up and putting her on the next ferry home. She was too different from the women of his world who knew the score.

Girls like Sara believed in happy ever after and white picket fences. If he took this relationship beyond the office, beyond the boundaries of Angel Island, it wouldn't be long before the gossip column hounds nipped at her heels and portrayed her as something she wasn't. He didn't want that for Sara.

Still, for the weekend she was his and if all it left him with was a memory to color his dreams at night, he'd take it.

Reluctantly, he released her. "Eat up. I want to show you the view from Mt Livermore."

JT pulled him aside out of hearing as Sara filled her plate. "You're taking her up Mt Livermore? A two and a half hour walk one way."

"Does that bother you because your date won't make it up there in her Jimmy Choos which means you'd have to stay here or do you not want me to be alone with Sara?"

"You're getting in too deep, my friend."

"I can't imagine it's her welfare you're concerned about, JT. You change women as often as you change your clothes."

"Yes, but those women know the score. Sara doesn't. And there's something about her that doesn't add up. She seems familiar. Like we've seen her somewhere before."

"Of course you have. In the short time she's worked for me, you've visited the office at least twice." He eased the niggle of doubt by justifying that he too had only really noticed Sara in the weeks leading up to his breakup with Giovanna. Not because she wasn't noticeable, but simply because she blended.

"What do you know about her really?"

"What do I need to know? She's beautiful, sexy, responsive and I feel at ease around her. She likes shrimp and oysters and picks the lettuce out of her salad. She is shy and intelligent, and I can hold a conversation with her." Not to mention that he was hooked on her curves. "She's the kind of girl who could fill the gap in my life. Is that what has you spooked, JT?" Carmelo's thoughts returned to their conversation on the yacht. "Are you afraid that if I close the door on my playboy reputation, yours will suffer too?"

There'd be no more wild bachelor parties. Life would become filled with civilized social events, babies, and backyard barbecues. The thought didn't scare him as much as he thought it would.

"That's not it, my friend. We've been through a lot together. You know me better than that. I am asking you to play it carefully. At least until we know a little more about this girl."

Carmelo turned to watch Sara as she cleared the table of leftovers from the meal. He could picture her pregnant with his child, and because that made him want to be alone with her again, he turned to JT.

"I see your point. We'd never be back in time for dinner at Indovinare."

"Why don't we head back to the yacht? The girls can catch a little sun on the bow and we can watch a re-run of the All-Star race at the Charlotte Speedway from a few years back. There's a car in there I'm looking to sponsor and the team has come up for sale." JT drained his flute of champagne and placed it on the table. "The driver is tipped to be a good investment."

"My back pocket is still hurting from the de la Cruz-Meira mess. Why would I want to invest in another team right now?" The thought of it made him shudder. No way would he tip his hand in only to have it burned again.

"I think you'll find the race finish of interest."

Carmelo caught JT's smug look but chose to ignore it. JT was being a pain in the ass. When he'd tried to raise the subject of Sara on their way up to the cafe, Carmelo had cut him short. Everything JT wanted to say about his involvement with her had already festered in the far reaches of Carmelo's mind. Nor did he want to sit in front of a television rehashing the technicalities of a race finish. For God's sake, was it too much to ask for a weekend away from business?

"I'd rather take a walk. Come, Sara. Since the

mountain walk is off the cards, we can take a stroll along the shore. See you back here in an hour, JT."

Carmelo ignored his friend's disapproval and captured her hand. The moment her fingers laced with his, tranquility flooded him. Her nearness alone took the edge off his mood. They strolled across the grass that led down to the sand in comfortable silence.

It was so good to not have incessant chatter in his ears, but there was a stiffness to Sara's back that had him wondering if JT's presence had irked her too. Getting away from him for a while had been a good idea for both of them. JT hadn't bothered to hide his distaste. Later Carmelo would deal with his friend's concerns. But now with Sara at his side, he wished the weekend wouldn't end so they didn't have to face reality on Monday.

He released her hand and drew her closer, placing his arm around her waist. She hesitated a little at first, but as their bodies moved together in silent agreement, she relaxed against him. Carmelo studied her beautiful face, the smooth skin caressing the gentle contours of her bones. He traced a finger across her cheek. She turned her face to him and smiled a soft, warm smile, and in that moment he lost a piece of his heart.

Reaching the shade of an old oak, he stopped within the privacy of the tree's great bulk to draw her into his arms. Inside him desperation mounted. With the taste of her lips only inches away, he needed to bury himself in her kiss and forget about the trials that awaited him on the mainland.

Her arms crept up his chest, encircled his neck and her body swayed towards his. His heart pounded knowing she wanted this as much as he did. She tilted her face, her lips parting on a sigh. Carmelo captured the sound with his mouth, lips searching, his tongue finding the warmth of hers.

Taking her weight, he pressed his back to the tree. She followed to position herself in the cradle of his hips. Oh God, she felt so good there. It seemed like forever since he'd loved every inch of her. And he wanted to do it again and again, until he'd exorcised these demons that haunted him.

His hands moved across her back, stroking, pressing her closer until there was no gap between them. He loved the feel of her curves under his palms, the taste of her on his lips. No one had ever made him feel the way Sara did. Something unrecognizable curled up from his gut. A feeling that went beyond desire but he didn't want to name it just yet.

Sara's breasts brushed his chest as she sank into him, her hips pressed into his and the unmistakable evidence of his arousal. Her groan shuddered through him, making him wish they were anywhere else but in a public place.

He pressed her to him with a hand on her incredibly sexy ass, the roundness of it a perfect fit in his palm. Lifting his mouth from hers, he whispered, "God, Sara, you drive me crazy. I need you."

Her hands left his shoulders to cup his face, her chestnut brown eyes fixed on his. She said nothing as she drew his head down and let her lips speak for her. Carmelo wanted her hands on his naked body in places where he could enjoy them to the fullest. He wanted to bury himself deep inside her and watch her face as she came under him. More than anything, he wanted to pleasure this woman who had set his soul free, even if only for a short moment in time.

He kissed a trail from her lips, across her cheek and along her jawline. She shuddered against him, her abdomen grazing the hard ridge behind the zipper on his cargo pants. Her hands slid inside the opening of his shirt, roaming every inch of the exposed skin. Everywhere she made contact, his skin heated with pleasure. Her fingers teased his nipple, sending his body into overdrive. He thrust against her making his desire known. The only thing stopping him from taking her right there was the sound of children's laughter and parent gossip invading their world and moving closer.

He held her hard against him, burying his face in her hair. "Later, baby," he whispered, unable to release her until the tempest inside him subsided.

Waiting for the group to pass by, he relinquished his hold on her and took her hands in his. Her cheeks were flushed with a bright shade of pink, her lips well and truly kissed. Carmelo's heart skipped a couple of beats at the thought he might never see that look again after tomorrow.

Chapter Eleven

Isadora watched the young family group pass by, saw the knowing smiles of the dads, the envious looks from the mums and the snickers from the kids as they hid behind their hands. Torn between mortification and frustration, she dipped her head and looked away. Carmelo tipped up her chin with a gentle finger and his gaze held hers until she forgot all about the rest of the world on Angel Island.

His eyes held a promise that made her forget her vendetta. Her intention had always been to destroy this man in return for destroying her career. Yet the deeper in and closer she got, the hungrier she became for the taste of him over the bittersweet flavor of revenge.

His palm cupped her face and she leaned into his hand. His eyes darkened with desire as he placed a soft, searching kiss on her lips. Then the warmth of his mouth was gone along with the heat of his body and the hard comfort of his length against her. He held her away and pushed up from the tree trunk.

"Let's get back to the yacht. I'd imagine Melissa is itching to swap her Jimmy Choos for a bikini and a manicure."

His teasing smile had Isadora's heart tumbling, a wicked grin that made her want to kiss him again, to feel that mouth curve over hers as it had only moments before.

She tore her eyes away. "Her name is Aylesha. And unless you have a manicurist stashed away on board, she'll have to wait until we reach the mainland."

They turned to walk back up the grass to the picnic tables where JT and Aylesha engaged in what looked to be a heated discussion. Earlier when JT had mentioned the Charlotte race, Isadora's heart had plummeted. He'd seen her tattoo, the one that had boldly been on display as she'd taken to the podium for her third-place win.

She hadn't released her hair from the ponytail after taking her helmet off and the cameraman had spotted it and zoomed in on the new etching. Everyone knew Hector de la Cruz's race car number, the trademark red helmet with three white stripes, and the dove symbolic of his freedom. Was that why JT suddenly wanted to watch the race again?

The terrifying thought that he'd recognized the tattoo made her nerves churn. She'd been a rookie in that race but she couldn't remember if JT was in the game back then. Carmelo had only come on the racing scene a year later looking for the opportunity to buy a team.

Carmelo's hand closed around hers, and the tension seeped away. Perhaps there was no reason at all to be on edge. Perhaps JT's concern had nothing to do with her or racing and everything to do with his best friend's wellbeing. She was his employee, and not Carmelo's usual style of date, so his lawyer had a right to be wary.

"Tell me, what does my beautiful assistant usually do for fun?" Carmelo's voice and the stroke of his thumb across the back of her hand drew Isadora from her thoughts.

She shivered at the fleeting touch that sent goosebumps rippling up her skin and made her body tighten with desire. If she didn't get a grip on this attraction to him, things could turn nasty really quickly. JT's antennae were already on high alert and as soon as he figured it out, the game would be up. Time was running out and she had to shut out the lover and focus on the man who'd destroyed her life.

"Not much." Isadora shrugged as she thought about pulling her hand from his, but it felt comfortable in his grip. She needed to draw on that strength to get her through the turmoil that would soon unravel and bring this moment to an end. "I hang out with my cat and watch old movies. Pretty boring stuff."

"A beautiful girl like you? No boyfriend, no dancing the night away in a club?"

A grueling training program and the need to stay ahead in the industry had been her focus until that day she'd been banned from racing, so parties had never been high on her agenda. Not that Isadora de la Cruz didn't like to party with the rest of them, but she had chosen the parties to attend and who she'd attended them with. But after Harlon's betrayal, she'd sworn never to be taken for a fool again.

"I like a little dancing, but I'm not a nightclub kinda girl." Unlike Carmelo who'd been seen in a few and partied hard.

"Hmm, I understand. The novelty wears off after a while. Now I prefer a slower kind of dance." His voice deepened as he leaned in and whispered in her ear, "Want to dance with me, Sara?"

The teasing glint in his eyes was one she hadn't seen before. It brought his eyes to life. There were so many different sides to this man, she wished she could spend a lifetime exploring them. But he wasn't hers to explore and when he found out the truth, he'd hate her for more than just losing his team a race.

Still, that look sent molten desire flying through her bloodstream and made her want to kiss him until that teasing glint turned to fire. She stopped walking and he turned to her, a frown forming on his brow. Damn it, if this was the last time she tasted his kiss, she'd make it count. Fear for what might happen next, despair that it would come before she achieved her goal, and pure white-hot lust drove her into his arms.

Isadora took his face between her palms, ran them along the shadow on his jaw, let her fingers trace the shell of his ears and tangle in the thickness of his hair. Then she brought his head down and rose up to press her lips to his, to taste the firm skin and feel the graze of day-old stubble against her face, a mix of heaven and torturous hell. How easy it would be to get drunk on the taste of that mouth and forget her purpose here at all.

"I want to dance with you," she whispered against his lips.

His arms came around her as he lifted her feet from the ground, body to body, breast to chest and everything in between. She wanted to be alone with him, to strip him bare and love every inch of him. Commit every taste, scent, and touch to senses she could raise on those cold, lonely nights ahead when all this would be a memory and pain replaced euphoria. All in the name of vengeance.

His kiss was hard and desperate, his mouth searching, his body clinging to hers as if he too knew that their time together was almost up. That this moment of madness in Paradise was at an end. One more night, that's all she wanted before she faced the harsh reality of the nightmare she'd created.

He set her on her feet, his breath coming fast against her hair. "Sweet Jesus, Sara. I can't get enough of you."

Her own breath came in spasms that burned in her chest. She blamed the prick of tears on the uneven rhythm of her heartbeat. How could a man who kissed like a god be the devil incarnate?

JT's voice came like a splash of cold water from behind Carmelo. "We need to get back to the yacht."

Over Carmelo's shoulder, Isadora caught his ice-cold look of disdain and averted her eyes from the accusations she saw there. JT Horne thought she was just another gold digger. She could only imagine what he'd think when he knew the truth.

Chapter Twelve

ilence filled the dinghy, a thick weighty fog that settled among them. JT's angry scowl accompanied the tight cross of his arms on his chest. Whatever had crawled up his ass this morning was biting hard now.

Aylesha studied the straps of her shoes and brushed at the remnants of grass on the heels, her face expressionless.

Carmelo shook his head. How had he not grown tired of the falseness before? Perhaps because he'd not cared to see it. Girls like Aylesha played the game. High level escorts who were willing bodies to warm their sheets, glittery accessories they carried on their arms who required no emotional involvement. In return the men they escorted got whatever they wanted. JT might be content with that for now, but Carmelo wasn't. Not anymore. Not since he'd kissed Sara.

In contrast to Aylesha's closed face, Sara's was lit with interest as he broke the heavy silence and told her the history of Angel Island. Her questions came hard and fast and tested his knowledge of the Bay. She might not be Californian-born, but she was a '49ers fan. That earned her a tick in his book.

She liked action movies and vintage Chevys, and her laugh was addictive. She could bait a hook and drop a crab net, and knew how to cook a mean Cajun shrimp, the sound of which made his mouth water. If he was the kind of man to fall in love, he'd choose Sara.

As the crew secured the dinghy, Carmelo helped her aboard. His mood had lifted and the smile wouldn't leave his lips as he watched her animated expressions. Aylesha headed for the cabin but JT hung back.

"I need a word with you," he said, ignoring the huff Aylesha gave when he didn't follow her down.

"Later," Carmelo said, his eyes on Sara and his mind already envisioning a lazy afternoon with her in his arms.

"No. Now."

The insistence in his voice raised a frown on Carmelo's brow. What could be so damn urgent it couldn't wait? This weekend was meant to be a break. Sara's gaze flicked to JT, and he saw uncertainty in them as she looked back at Carmelo. He sighed. JT wouldn't rest until he'd cleared whatever was on his mind.

"I'll go downstairs and freshen up." With a nervous look at JT, she turned and walked away.

JT's hand on Carmelo's arm drew his attention away from the sway of her hips and the wicked thoughts the movement raised.

"You've got it bad, buddy. This isn't wise."

"Why can't you leave it alone?"

"Do you really need me to spell it out for you? She is so far out of your league, man."

Carmelo sighed. "I'm not even sure I have a league anymore."

"I'm telling you there's something wrong here. Aylesha reckons she's seen her on the circuit."

"So maybe she has. Maybe she likes racing too. There are millions of NASCAR fans in America who do." He ran a frustrated hand through his hair. He didn't want to hear any of it.

"What about the tattoo on her neck?"

"What about it?"

"It's a racing helmet. And it's familiar. I've seen it somewhere before."

Carmelo cocked an eyebrow at him. "Are you messing with me? She's a '49ers fan. It could be a football helmet."

JT shook his head. "It's too detailed not to mean something. I'll do some research on it."

Carmelo's patience with his friend began to wear thin. "Let me get this straight … you're going to research a tattoo just to make some point because your girlfriend thinks she's seen Sara somewhere before? I'd suggest you put your time to better use. Like finding something constructive to do. Start by keeping your girlfriend busy so her mind is filled with something other than her next manicure and idle gossip. Or watch that rerun of the race and see if it's really worth the investment."

"So I must be the business mind while you go down there and —"

Carmelo held up his hand, anger whipping up from deep in his gut. "Don't you dare say what I think you're about to. We've been friends a long time, JT. I respect you. I respect your mind and your choices. And your opinion. I know you have a problem with Sara, with me, with this situation. Right now, she is my choice. I know what I'm doing."

"Do you, Carmelo? If she is the innocent you think she is, you will destroy that girl for the sake of a few hours' pleasure. You think you've changed, but you haven't. She's not like the others. And if she is like the others, she *will* destroy you."

In his mind Carmelo knew JT was right, but his heart and body had other ideas. Downstairs in his cabin was a woman who was warm and inviting, not an ulterior motive in sight. She wanted him and he wanted her right back. Tomorrow could take care of itself. Tonight was for him and Sara.

"I know," he said, and left JT to his unwelcome theories.

Downstairs, he found her in his cabin, naked under the covers, her lashes resting on damp cheeks. Her hand gripped the sheet in a fist against her breasts and she lay on her side with her creamy shoulders exposed to his touch.

Carmelo skimmed a lazy path down her arm with his fingers and captured her hand beneath his. Kneeling beside the bed, he pressed a kiss to her shoulder. She stirred under his touch. His lips followed the caresses down her arm. Turning her hand over in his, he nipped at the pulse point on her wrist. She rolled over onto her back and her hands found his hair, soothing on his scalp as they eased away the tension.

"Hey," he whispered.

"Hey," she answered, her smile sleepy and a little sad.

JT's warnings slipped away as Carmelo took in her beautiful face, those warm brown eyes and her mouth that beckoned to his. He released her hands and stood, wanting to be as naked as she was, to feel the satin of her skin against his, the touch of her hands on his body.

She pushed herself up on her elbows, the sheet slipping away to reveal breasts his hands itched to caress. Her eyes followed every movement as he stripped down, the heat in her gaze building. God help him, he was lost in Sara. His heart pounded, desire mounting, his body responding to the reach of her hands, and then he was beside her, her arms embracing him, her breasts pressed to his chest.

Carmelo kissed her slowly, taking time to enjoy the taste of her, a drug he was fast becoming hooked on. Her fingers played along his spine, her palms stroked the muscles of his hips and ass. He cursed the barrier of silk sheets between them because he needed to feel all of her, every gorgeous inch filling his hands.

A lock of hair fell across her face as her mouth slipped from the kiss to press into the curve of his neck. He tucked it behind her ear.

"You're sad." He hadn't forgotten the trace of tears on her cheeks.

She nodded. "A little."

"Is it JT?"

Her sigh feathered along his skin. "JT. Us. This." Her kiss was little more than a whisper against his pulse. "Tomorrow."

"Let tomorrow take care of itself." He rolled onto his back, lifted his ass, and pushed the sheets down. "We'll work through this."

She turned on her side, balancing on her elbow, palm under her chin. Her free hand traced the dips and curves of his shoulders, caressed the smattering of hair on his chest before following a line down to his navel.

"I shouldn't be here. I should have left after the party. I can't get enough of you. That scares me. What will we do when Monday comes?"

Carmelo raised his hand to cup her face, traced her lips with his thumb, shivered as she nipped at the pad. "No regrets, remember? Come here." With a hand on her hip, he guided her over his body and settled her in the cradle of his hips. She moved against him, her back arched, and all he could think of was being inside her. "I meant what I said. Your job is safe."

His hands found those beautiful breasts, drew one to his lips, caressed it, suckled on the generous pink nipple then paid equal attention to the other. The moist heat of Sara's body on his and the movement of her hips against him had his hands racing over her back to cup her hips. He pressed her down, thrust up, ready for her but Sara wasn't finished with him yet.

Her lips sparked a trail of fire down his chest, her hand slipping between them to take him, the smooth skin of her palm working a magic, a connection, he'd never experienced before. But he had no desire to compare her with previous lovers. He simply knew there'd never be another like her and that scared him.

Then her lips replaced her hands, control and coherent thought was taken from him as he writhed beneath her and tried to hold on to his sanity. His hands tangled in her hair, desperate to keep her there or tear her away, he no longer knew what he needed. She raised herself over him, taking all of him inside her warmth until all he could feel around him was Sara, possessing his body and his mind.

Her hips began a dance he was happy to participate in. This time he couldn't tear his gaze from her face, couldn't close his eyes to the beauty of this woman. Her head fell back, the blonde waves cascading down her back as she rode him into mindless oblivion. He held her hips as they came in harmony, embraced her as she collapsed on his chest and wondered at the damp tears on the skin over his heart. Then he rubbed her back until they slept — exhausted, satiated.

Chapter Thirteen

Carmelo's heart beat steadily under Isadora's ear, his breathing even as he slept and her tears fell against his skin. She'd defied logic sleeping with him, not just once but twice. She hated herself for enjoying it. Hated him for being the perfect lover. Hated that she'd have to face up to the truth that they were not meant for each other.

Her plan had derailed and she'd lost sight of her goal. The injustices she'd fought for had paled in comparison to the pleasure of being skin on skin with Carmelo. The race, the loss, his involvement in the outcome and the humiliation of disqualification no longer existed in this fantasy world they'd created here out in the middle of the Bay. Instead it had morphed into a much bigger problem.

God forgive her, she'd fallen in love with the enemy.

And when it came time to reveal her true identity, it would shatter the fragile glass dome they'd created and tear them to shreds with the shards of her deception. He'd never trust her again because she'd lied to him. Pretended to be someone she wasn't, intent on taking him down, making him pay. Instead, she'd be the one to pay. Isadora de la Cruz had lost again. But this time the cost could not be counted in dollars and cents.

"I'm sorry," she whispered, pressing her lips to his throat before snuggling deeper into him. She would enjoy the weight of his arms around her, feel the strength of his body beneath hers and know that for this moment in time he belonged only to her. His chest rose and fell with the steady breath of sleep. Isadora placed her hand over his heart and closed her eyes.

She awoke to a darkened cabin and the sound of raised voices. Beside her the silk sheets were cold and empty. Premonition weighed heavily in the pit of her stomach. Above deck, an argument took place that had Carmelo and JT trading insults loud enough to be heard from the mainland.

Isadora searched for her clothes and found them, a dark pile on a chair in the corner of the cabin. On the table next to the bed, the digital clock showed 7 p.m., the red glow eerie in the semi-darkness.

She scooted across the sheets and grabbed hold of

her clothes, tugging them on quickly. Outside the shouting escalated. Her heart pounded as she heard JT shout her name. Isadora de la Cruz. It stopped dead at the knock on the cabin door.

Isadora ran a hand through the tangled mess of her hair, her stomach churning. Tentatively, she reached for the handle and opened the door.

Aylesha lounged against the wall, nail file in hand, casually shaping the already pointed tips of her nails. She looked up, her eyes cold and her smile mean.

"I guess no one told you never to shit on your own doorstep."

Isadora wanted to slap the smirk from her face, except she had a point.

Aylesha pushed away from the wall, flicked her hair over her shoulder and slipped her feet into her sparkling silver Jimmy Choo pumps. "Show's on and you're the star. I've been told to come and get you. You're going down, *Isadora*."

Bile rose in Isadora's throat as her great plan for revenge unraveled at her feet. She had nothing on Carmelo yet, and he had everything on her, courtesy of his lawyer. Every instinct screamed that he knew the truth, that JT Horne had gone looking and found everything he needed to know. That he'd recognized the tattoo, watched the race in Charlotte and got the confirmation he needed.

Shoes in hand, she followed Aylesha down the

corridor to the stairs leading up to the deck. Ice-cold sweat trickled down her spine, guilt a boulder in her stomach. She'd become the enemy and she wasn't in friendly waters. Isadora stumbled at the base of the stairs, her heart pounding. Carmelo's voice drifted down.

"You've got it wrong, JT. I'm sure there's a perfectly reasonable explanation."

"For Christ's sake, man, open your eyes. She's played you for a fool."

Aylesha turned, her plump red lips forming a smirk. "You thought you were so smart sleeping with Carmelo. Just like you did with Harlon. Looks like you're the one who got screwed." She placed a foot on the first step, hands on her hips. "You should have been a little more careful. The track is a very small world. You took Harlon from me, now I take Carmelo from you."

Isadora closed her eyes and swallowed the sob that rose in her throat. It all made perfect sense now — the look of hatred in Aylesha's eyes, the barbed comments on the island and her coldness towards Isadora.

"You're another one of Harlon's girls. He had quite a record with the race girls and so many to choose from. His own personal dating pool." A fact Isadora had only found out when it was too late. Or maybe she'd been naive enough to think she could be different. "You were one in a line of many." And it riled Isadora too that she'd become a statistic. Just as she was about to become a statistic again, this time in Carmelo's life.

The smirk on Aylesha's face turned to a sneer. "But you had more than just me for competition. When it got too hot for Harlon Meira, he ran home to his wife."

The barb found a home in her heart. "He sure kept *that* a closely guarded secret." No one in the race circles had known his wife existed, but once they did, the scandal of what had occurred in the pit garage at Iannello Racing had unraveled into a tangled mess of cheating, lies and false accusations.

"I knew, but it didn't matter. Wives who won't follow their man around the track shouldn't be surprised when they fool around. But *you*, Isadora, you changed Harlon. I won't let you change Carmelo. So now you must meet your fate."

Isadora shuddered at the hatred in Aylesha's tone. Perhaps the silly girl had really loved Harlon. God help her, Isadora had too until she'd realized he was a two-timing race cheat.

She'd been tripped up by an unexpected enemy as Harlon's reputation came back to haunt her. But he was the least of her concerns now as above deck, JT drove the final nail into her cross.

"Ask her, Carmelo. Ask her what her *real* name is."

With a mocking glance, Aylesha moved up the stairs and onto the deck, leaving Isadora no choice but to follow. Her mind might not be as empty as Isadora had first thought, but her claws were as sharp as expected.

Stepping out into the evening shadows, lights twinkled all around the bay. To the left, the dark eerie shape of Alcatraz mocked her. She too was a prisoner of her own lies.

Her gaze shifted to Carmelo where he stood on deck, arms folded. His eyes narrowed on her, searching. JT paced, his feet stilling as she approached. On the table between them, a laptop glowed with the results of a search engine bearing Isadora de la Cruz's name.

Isadora hardly recognized the girl in the picture. She seemed so far removed from who she'd become. The only similarity they shared was the tattoo of a dove on a helmet, clearly displayed in a profile shot in third place on the podium.

Numbness crept through her from her feet up. She didn't feel the sting of the cool breeze as it picked up, didn't hear the slap of water against the hull. Her gaze slid back to Carmelo's face and found his expression unreadable. Gone was the heat and desire, in its place a cold and stony wall.

Carmelo reached out to swivel the laptop so Isadora could see the full results of the search. She looked away from him to the screen. Images of her and her father, her first race, first win, the go-kart she'd learned to race in. Her father's car — the eighties relic that had made him a star — his helmet and the dove that symbolized his freedom and hard work to become one of America's top racing car drivers.

Anger seethed from him, and Isadora couldn't blame him. Instead of plotting revenge, she should have confronted Carmelo with the truth from the start. But she'd followed the path of retribution because she couldn't trust anyone to tell her the truth. Needed to find the truth herself. There had been too many lies already. Tears pricked at her lids. She blinked them back. She hadn't counted on falling in love.

"You have some explaining to do. Start with your real name, *Miss Stewart*." Carmelo moved closer, his height and size intimidating, his body language demanding she meet his gaze so he could pick out any lies she might tell.

Isadora folded her arms across her torso to ward off the chill that came from within, her eyes dropping to the screen and the picture of her and her father together during the happiest time of her life. "My name is Isadora Sara Stewart de la Cruz. I am Isadora de la Cruz."

Carmelo thrust his hands through his hair, a movement she'd come to recognize as frustration. Her heart contracted, squeezing her chest with a pain so sharp it had her drawing in a breath. She wanted him to shout at her, shake her ... something, anything that would make him look at her. He didn't.

"Why?" he thundered.

"Why what? Why did I lie? Why did I take the job? Why did I—" She couldn't bring herself to say the words. She'd cheapened herself by sleeping with him, weakened her plan for revenge because she'd felt something deeper for him than anger. But she'd found something in his arms she'd never expected. Warmth and caring, and a sense of belonging.

"Start with your reason for lying about who you are," Carmelo demanded, turning his back on her to face the bay.

"You tried to fix the race at Daytona Beach. Look at me, damn you. Look at me and deny it to my face."

"I had nothing to do with what happened." He gripped the railing, his back, and shoulders stiff, but stayed looking out across the water.

"You knew adding a polyurethane bushing to the stabilizers was illegal. That it would give me more control and a quicker response, an advantage over those using solids. A means to win the race with a banned modification."

Carmelo shook his head. "I heard that was your idea. You and Harlon Meira set that up between you."

"Why would I do that? I had the skill to win without it. Harlon said you ordered it, that you had money down on your own team." Isadora stepped toward him, her hand out to reach for his arm, to make him face her, to look her in the eyes and tell her the truth.

He shrugged off her hand, his knuckles white, his

lips drawn in a grim line. "Harlon Meira is a liar. And so are you." His quiet words fell like stones on the water, sending ripples of despair through her.

"I didn't fix that race, Carmelo. I wanted to win it on my own merit, fair and square. For my dad, Hector de la Cruz. He died during a race rollover at Daytona Beach. That was the track that killed him." Desperation brought the tightness of tears to her throat. "I wasn't lying about how he died. I needed to win that race for my dad, to take home the cup in the de la Cruz name. I wanted to put our name on the winner's board for him. It should have been his name up there, claiming victory for the race that killed him. But you stole that from me with your greed for money."

"We weren't the greedy ones. You were. We didn't fix that race. We knew nothing of the money or the odds. And we certainly didn't order any modifications to the car." Carmelo turned and slammed the laptop closed. "What was your purpose here, Isadora? Blackmail? Extortion? Did you think that by sleeping with me you could buy me off?"

"I came for the truth. You stole my dream, fired me from the team. I took the fall for the Boys' Club so you could walk away with a clean nose and now I can never race again. I wanted to find the proof that you fixed that race so I could clear my name."

"And then what?" He towered over her, his bulk intimidating.

Isadora drew herself up to face him and stood her ground. "Then I'd use it to bring you down, to expose you for the race fixing you tried to pin on me."

"That's not true." Carmelo didn't need to raise his voice. His anger spoke for him, but it was the ice in his voice that froze her heart, numbing the pain of betrayal. "JT, I'd like to talk to Isadora alone."

"I don't think that's a good idea." JT's look of disdain rattled her nerves. "As your lawyer, I should be present for this."

"You're not here as my lawyer, you're here as my friend. Please respect our friendship and do as I ask."

"This is a mistake, Carmelo."

"Then it's my mistake to make."

The stilted words between the men made Isadora want to run from this nightmare of her own creation. What did it matter anymore? Even if she succeeded in clearing her name, no one would hire her on their team again after this new scandal emerged. The damage had been done. Her sacrifice had been for nothing.

Her gaze drifted to Aylesha, who appeared openly delighted by Isadora's discomfort. She'd love to wipe that smirk off the girl's face, except she deserved the ridicule. It turned out she was smarter than Isadora had given her credit for after all. She should never have accepted Carmelo's invitation, never have let her attraction to him interfere with her goal, never have let him get under her skin and be fooled by his charm. She'd repeated the mistakes of her past.

"Fine, but this is on your head, Carmelo." JT turned to walk into the cabin. Come, Aylesha." His girlfriend followed him reluctantly, the look on her face pure bitch.

Then she and Carmelo were alone. Isadora waited for the rage she deserved, the explanation she was no longer sure she wanted. Had she been so duped by Harlon Meira that she'd almost taken down an innocent man, almost destroyed his business for nothing?

"I trusted you. Yet you didn't trust me … after everything we've shared … Why didn't you come to me?" Carmelo's words were barely audible above the lap of waves against the hull of the yacht.

"There was no point. I'd been set up to take the fall. I didn't have anything to do with the plan to throw the race, I swear. Winning meant too much to me."

"You lied to me. You set out to infiltrate my business, dig up dirt and feed me to the sharks, all on the hearsay of a man who is as big a liar as you. I trusted you with a secret I'd never told anyone except my closest, most valued friends." He pushed his hands through his hair, his gaze focused on the Bay. "Did you ever, for one moment, spare a thought for the fact that you might have it wrong? That I had nothing to do with fixing that race."

Isadora twisted her hands and shivered in the cold

evening air. Carmelo turned to face her, his eyes empty of passion and full of anger. She wanted to turn back the clock and undo everything that had taken place — her father's death, the race, the cheating, and the mistake of sleeping with Carmelo. Yet even now, as he stood against the backdrop of San Francisco's skyline, a dark and sexy silhouette, seething with disparagement, she loved him.

Tears slipped down her cheeks. She dashed them away. Self-loathing ached in her throat. She'd never given thought to the fact that maybe Carmelo was as much a victim in this as she was.

Chapter Fourteen

She stood shivering in the night, but his beautiful Sara was gone. In her place stood Isadora de la Cruz, the woman who had destroyed his name then slept with him and stolen a piece of his heart.

"You're good. I'll give you that." His words fell quietly between them. "Not many people fool me, but you did." To the point of making him fall completely, blindly, and stupidly in love with her. "It humiliates me to admit that JT was right. You lied to me just like all the others. You cared more about money and exacting revenge than you did about me. I believed your lies, your sweet and innocent ways, and when we made love, I believed you were enjoying it every bit as much as I was. But you faked it, didn't you?"

"No."

Her denial stirred his anger higher. "Everything you

stand for is a *lie*. Out of all that has happened since that race, *this* is the ultimate humiliation. You got what you wanted, *Isadora*. I've paid the price for blackmailing you to come aboard my yacht, for believing you were no one other than Sara Stewart, my quiet, unassuming assistant. But she's a fake, isn't she? Behind the mask was Isadora de la Cruz whose goal it was to win, whatever the stakes." The taste of betrayal and deception lay bitter on his tongue. "How much?"

Her head jerked up, the glint of tears in her eyes caught in the soft lighting from the party lights wrapped around the upper deck railing. He wouldn't let his heart be swayed by tears.

"It's not about money."

Even to his own ears, his laugh was as bitter as the air in the Bay in winter. "It's *always* about money."

"This time it's about justice. It's hard enough being a woman in a man's world, always trying to prove oneself worthy, never quite reaching the same level of appreciation, always having to fight for a place on the podium. Then to go out on a scandal like Daytona Beach, knowing you're taking the fall—"

"I wasn't responsible for what happened at Daytona Beach. You and Harlon Meira were partners." The thought made him ill until he reminded himself who she was; a woman who would cheat on another man's wife. "There was a substantial amount of money on that race. Harlon told me it was your idea to change the suspension. That you blackmailed him into it, threatened to tell his wife about the affair if he didn't make a plan for you to win."

"That's not true! I didn't even know he had a wife. If I had, I would never have gotten involved with the lying, cheating asshole." Her anger rolled across the deck. "I told you before I had the skill and the drive to win on my own merit. Harlon had a problem with money. I had no idea how big a problem until I checked my bank account to find he'd taken what was left of my savings with him when he high-tailed it back to Georgia. The portion he hadn't squandered on race bets in my name."

Carmelo's heart wanted to believe her, but his head was in charge due to it and other body organs being unreliable witnesses. "So that's why we found betting tickets with your name on them? Is this just another lie? The race purse was one million dollars. The betting payout would have been twice that if you'd won. You and Harlon had a lot to gain."

"I don't gamble. I don't bet on races. I drive to win. Not for the money or the glory, but because I can. There was only one reason to win that race and that was to honor my father and the dreams he didn't get to fulfill." She hugged her arms around her waist. "I didn't place those bets. Harlon did. On *your* instructions. Then when the race board found out about the suspension changes, you blamed me, and Harlon let you."

That she thought he was capable of something so despicable pained him. "Either you're a damn good liar or Harlon Meira was. Let me tell you something, Isadora ... I've worked hard to build my life from nothing so I'm not a gambling man. My parents fought their way through life trying to make ends meet, to make a living for themselves in the lucky country and provide a comfortable, loving home in which to raise their family. But still we had very little to live on and their dreams went unfulfilled with a son to raise and ill health a black dog at their door. By sixteen I was an orphan out on the streets. Do you think I would gamble away my success to return to those times again? No! But all anyone sees now is the success I've become and the money that comes with it."

He moved back to the rail and the view of the city. He couldn't bear to look at her anymore. The memory of her warmth in his arms, her body against his and her delectable mouth teasing his skin faded, swallowed by the anger that burned within him. "You played me for a fool. You're no better than the others."

"I will say this again. I had nothing to do with fixing the race."

He heard her words but wasn't in the mood to believe them. "Neither did I."

Her footsteps sounded on the deck and suddenly she stood close. He focused on the mainland, not wanting to be swayed by her beauty or the pleading in her eyes.

Because that's what women like her did. They played a man for a fool then took everything he owned. She wouldn't get everything, but he'd give her something. "Three million dollars."

"*What*?"

Who knew one word could carry so much disgust? But he could no longer believe anything that rolled off her traitorous tongue. "That's my offer. Take it or leave it. JT will do the leg work on an investigation and, if you're telling the truth, I'll give you a public apology clearing your name in the race-fixing scandal, and one more chance on the team to restore your reputation. Win or lose, you're out, but you'll have a better chance of racing again with another team. You have until Phoenix to get back into shape." He eyed her curves with a sneer on his lips while his heart ached over having to let her go.

"I am telling the *truth*. That's what I'm trying to prove. You think money will make this go away?"

The need to hurt her as much as she'd hurt him burned deep in his belly. "Isn't that what you came for, *Isadora*? If not as compensation then consider it payment for services rendered. You're a damn good lay. You should consider it as a career."

"You bastard." The sting of her palm on his cheek had him taking a step back. She followed him, took his face in her hands, and kissed the insults out of his mouth.

Her hands burned an imprint on his cheeks, her lips punished his until he tasted blood — hers or his, he couldn't tell. His hands found her hips and dragged her closer until she could feel his need for her. He ground his lower body against her, pressing into her like a rutting ram, intent on humiliating her, but in turn humiliating himself.

Then she bit down hard on his lip and called him a name that was the same insult in every language across the world. Before he could retaliate, she'd pulled out of his arms and was halfway across the deck.

"See you in Phoenix."

Then she was gone, swallowed by the inner recesses of his yacht. He pulled the handkerchief from his pocket and dabbed at his lip, wincing as the cloth came away red with blood. *Que Sera*.

Climbing the ladder to the pilot house, he ordered the captain to take the yacht back to the club mooring then poured himself a whiskey and watched the lights of San Francisco draw nearer.

Chapter Fifteen

I sadora had never felt pain quite like this before.
Not even when her dad died. It was as if the devil
himself had reached in and ripped out her soul.
Her chest contracted, tight enough to restrict her
breathing. Her head ached and her lips throbbed from
the assault on Carmelo's.

She let herself cry. Great, heaving sobs muffled by
the downy softness of Carmelo's pillow. It would take
the maid a few washes to get the makeup off the cover
and that gave her a margin of satisfaction. No matter
how small the victory, she had destroyed something of
Carmelo's. Except the victory was bittersweet because
she was still the loser.

Deep in the hull of the yacht, the engines throbbed
to life. Soon they'd be back at the club. She'd go home
to her apartment and this would be yet another

humiliation to put behind her. The cost? Her heart. Because no matter how cruel Carmelo might be now, she'd fallen in love with the side of him she'd seen this weekend.

Even though he didn't believe her, he'd given her a second chance. He'd have to do a press release about her racing for the team at Phoenix which in the eyes of the press would equal an apology, an exemption. It would restore her reputation enough to gain a second chance on another team — maybe. If she could find one that would take her.

With Carmelo's three million dollars she could start her own team. Except she wouldn't take his money. Never. Isadora had every intention of returning his check if he tried to give it to her. If she won the race in Phoenix, she'd have a good start with the race purse alone. Fair and square. Carmelo's team would be new. Harlon's crew had quit after he'd gone back to Georgia. She could make this work. It was all that was left of her dream.

Isadora lifted her head at a tap at the door. She wiped away the remnants of tears with her fingers.

"Excuse me, Miss Stewart?" Maria opened the door a crack. "I have your clothes."

The humiliation was complete. The vintage dress she'd worn last night would now forever be a reminder of her stupidity. "Thanks, Maria."

The maid stepped into the room and placed the

clothes on the edge of the bed. With a discreet look at Isadora's face, she went into the bathroom to return with a warm, damp cloth. "Here we go. I'll bring you a nice cup of tea. We'll be arriving at the club in about half an hour."

With a sad smile and a nod, Maria left Isadora alone. How many of Carmelo's women had she done that for in the past? How many pillow covers had she thrown away because they carried the stain of discarded lovers?

Fifteen minutes later, Isadora shed the capri pants and crop top, showered and was back in her own clothes, sipping a hot cup of tea. By the time the yacht reached the mooring, she'd scrubbed every inch of distress from her face and reapplied her mask, but all trace of Sara Stewart was gone from her soul. In Sara's place, Isadora de la Cruz prepared to face her adversaries.

Isadora opened the door to find Aylesha moving down the corridor towards the exit. With a self-satisfied smirk, the woman stopped to gloat.

"Free ride's come to an end, Isadora." Isadora hated the way Aylesha hissed her name. Like the snake she was. "Watch your back in Phoenix. Carmelo let you off lightly. You might not be so lucky next time."

Every instinct made her want to bite back, but she held her tongue. If it was hard to fit in as a driver, it was harder still to break into the brat pack of track girls. Isadora had no desire to be part of their little club, but the damage they could do had far reaching results as Aylesha had proved today. The best she could hope for was that Aylesha didn't make the cut for track girl on race day. She silently wished her a plague of pimples and a bout of stomach flu as she breezed past her up onto the deck.

Her heart stuttered when she spotted Carmelo at the rail. His jaw was set with a grim expression and his lip a little swollen. A shaft of regret flashed through her at the sight of his handsome face. If things had been different she would have walked up, stood close and let her hands wander over the muscles in his arms, stop to caress his narrow waist, and draw him into an embrace. But that was a lifetime ago now.

Isadora straightened her shoulders, stiffened her spine, and dredged up the courage that had gone missing this weekend. She moved to where the skipper waited to assist them from the yacht. As she reached Carmelo, he held out a white envelope. Isadora stared at it, her cheeks glowing red as disgust rose in her throat.

"Take it," he said, looking at a point over her head somewhere on the far horizon.

"I don't want it." She clenched her fists at her side, knowing the envelope would contain a check for the three million dollars he'd offered her. She searched his face in the light from the jetty. His hand covered hers and for a moment her heart pounded with hope that he'd want to talk this through, listen to what she had to say, believe that she'd had no involvement in Harlon's schemes. Instead, he stuffed the envelope into her hand and closed her fingers around it then stepped away as if he couldn't bear to be in the same breathing space.

She wanted to throw it back at him, tear it up and toss it into the Bay, but the warning look in his eyes stopped her. Isadora slipped the envelope into her purse where it would stay. "You'll be waiting a long time for me to cash it. It's not your money I want or need."

"Then you're a fool. Joe will be waiting to take you home." He nodded stiffly to the skipper who held out a hand to help her into the motorboat that would take her ashore. "You may clean out your desk on Monday."

And that was it. It was over. Just like that. She had her job back on his team, but she was no longer his assistant. She had one race to prove herself and an apology forthcoming. She'd won. Yet there was no victory in defeating him. Only the hollow success of an unknown future.

After an interminably long ride back in the motorboat, her feet finally tapped out an uneven rhythm on the wooden dock. Beside her, the skipper took long strides she didn't even try to keep up with. JT and Aylesha had stayed behind so she was spared their mocking company on her walk of shame. Around her the Bay was alive with nightlife. Laughter, chatter, and fun. All while inside her a little of her heart died with each step. She envied them their freedom.

Joe, God bless him, stood waiting with the door of the car open. Isadora bent her head and let her hair cover her profile so he couldn't see the tears that pricked at her eyes at the sight of a familiar and friendly face. But he knew. The gentle pat on her shoulder as he helped her into the seat was enough to make the tears slip down her cheeks.

He closed the door and she heard the rumble of a brief conversation before Joe slid behind the wheel and started the motor. It purred to life and he turned around in the seat. "There's a decanter of brandy on the shelf to your right. Help yourself."

Isadora hiccupped over a sob. "No, thank you, Joe."

Joe let out a sigh. "I warned you about him, Sara. No good could ever come of it."

"You did." She lay her head back on the soft leather and closed her eyes, letting the smooth rumble of the motor wash over her and the tears fall.

Joe set the car in motion. "You might as well spill it. No point bottling it up now."

And because Joe was her friend and it didn't matter because he'd find out anyway, she told him everything. Everything except for those private moments with Carmelo. Those were memories she wanted to keep for the long cold nights when she lay alone in bed with only the cat for company.

Joe whistled his disbelief through his teeth. "That's a fine mess you've got yourself into, young lady." He pulled up outside her apartment at the top of the crooked street. Was it only yesterday he'd picked her up from there?

"I know."

"Well, good luck in Phoenix. I'll be cheering you on from in front of my television screen." He stepped out of the car and came around to open the door.

Isadora eased out and adjusted her skirt then reached out to give him a hug. "Thanks for listening."

He hugged her back. "Stay in touch, Isadora Sara Stewart de la Cruz." He grinned at her in the light of the streetlamp. "You've got my number if you need an ear."

She smiled sadly. Her only friend in the world besides her cat was the enemy's chauffeur. If she stayed in touch with Joe, she'd only have to hear of Carmelo's latest business venture or worse, his latest girlfriend. Still, she thanked him again. He waited until she closed the apartment building security gate behind her before getting back into the car and driving away.

As Isadora opened her purse to retrieve her apartment key, her fingers touched the envelope. The pay off. She wondered if Carmelo had included a bonus for the great sex. Snapping the bag shut, she thrust the key into the lock, opened the door and stepped inside to flick on the light switch. Warm light flooded the apartment.

Cruzer lay curled up on his favorite chair, his only greeting a soft meow. Through the open curtains of the sitting room, lights glowed around the city. Inside the apartment, silence screamed loneliness. Isadora opened her purse again to retrieve the envelope. He hadn't even sealed it.

She tossed the purse onto the hallway table and walked to the liquor cabinet, stopping a moment to scratch behind Cruzer's ears and enjoy the comfort of his satisfied purr.

She opened the doors and placed the envelope on the shelf against a bottle of whiskey then poured an Irish liqueur. Carmelo's handwriting taunted her. Strong black strokes, confident like him. A little angry given the depth of the imprint on the paper. Isadora pushed open the flap on the envelope and drew out a company check made out in her full legal name. She'd been bought and sold for three million dollars ... and a bonus of five hundred thousand. Tossing the envelope aside, she abandoned the glass and drank the liqueur straight from the bottle until the burn of alcohol killed the pain.

On Sunday, she didn't bother getting out of bed. Instead she cried until there was nothing left inside except numbness. Her muscles ached from being curled up in a ball all day. No doubt her eyes were puffy and her nose was glowing red too, except she was too exhausted to check the mirror. Beside her, the empty tissue box paid testimony to her distress.

On the table next to the bed, her father stared out from the photograph taken at a race win, his eyes alight with victory. She could almost hear his voice in the room. "Get up, *chiquita*. Don't let those bastards win. To be beaten it means you did not fight back."

And her dad knew all about fighting back. They'd fought their way through life, just the two of them, her mother a ghost of a memory. They'd risen through the ranks of racing together and then he'd fought as long as he could against his injuries. She owed it to him, if no one else, to drag herself out of bed and start all over.

Isadora lifted the frame and pressed a kiss to the cold glass before putting it back down again. Next to it, the gym pass card that had been in the envelope with Carmelo's check reminded her that she had a job to do. She may no longer be his assistant or his lover but she still had access to *Fit to Race*'s state-of-the-art gym as his team driver. And she'd start tomorrow.

Chapter Sixteen

Sunday passed in oblivion. Carmelo had never been one to drown his sorrows, but he'd finished a bottle of whiskey the night before that had left him with a pounding hangover and Isadora's betrayal still fresh in his mind.

He'd wanted to numb the ache, to forget all about her, but couldn't. Her presence was everywhere in his cabin — the perfume spritzer she'd left behind, the clothes he'd bought her dumped in the trash can, the strands of blonde hair on his silk sheets and the remnants of her tears on his pillow.

JT had dropped Aylesha at home and driven back to talk about his decision to put Isadora back on the team.

It was hard to think of her as Isadora de la Cruz when his heart only wanted to identify with her as Sara.

Perhaps if he could say her real name out loud, he wouldn't feel the crushing weight on his chest.

It didn't matter who she was, she'd betrayed him. Twenty-four hours later it still stung that, as he'd watched her leave, she'd taken a piece of his soul with her.

Women were all the same. They came, they took, they left. How could he ever have expected Sara to be different?

Carmelo placed the empty glass on the table and looked across at JT. The Bloody Mary had eased the hangover and hopefully the painkillers would do the rest. "That's my decision."

JT looked at him in astonishment. "You paid her three and a half million dollars and still gave her another chance on the team? She must have been a good f—"

Carmelo sent him a warning look that stopped JT in his tracks. It didn't matter that he was right. She was everything he'd ever wanted in a woman. "I want a full investigation launched into Harlon Meira's activities. And if there is enough evidence, I'll bring criminal charges against him."

JT shoved his hands into the pockets of his suit trousers. "What about Miss de la Cruz?"

And therein lay the dilemma. Carmelo could accept her denial or he could have her investigated too. But what was the point? Once she'd raced in Phoenix, he'd never see her again. He'd sell the team and pull out of racing. Concentrate on *Fit to Race* and the clothing lines instead. But if what she'd told him was the truth, he owed it to her to bring Harlon Meira to justice for his actions.

"Let's start with Meira."

JT frowned. "I disagree. She was clearly on a mission to ruin your business and you can't let her off lightly, my friend."

"I know you want blood, JT. But we play this one my way."

"I think you're making a mistake." JT shrugged. "But, if that's what you really want, I'll get someone onto it first thing in the morning. I guess you'll be looking for another assistant?"

"Seems that way." The thought didn't inspire him the way it should.

"I know just the guy for the job — Mike's partner, Greg. I heard he's on the hunt for an assistant's position." JT paused to study him a moment. "She really got to you, didn't she?"

She had. In a way no woman ever had before. Carmelo waited for the anger to resurface, but it didn't. In its place a void formed, a vacuum of emptiness. A life of existence rather than living.

He twirled the drinking glass with his fingers, the lights of the Bay reflected in the crystal etchings. "She had me fooled."

"I tried to warn you. The moment I saw that tattoo, I

knew she was a fake."

Carmelo grimaced. "Like there's nothing fake about your girlfriend."

JT sighed. "I hear you. But at least what I see is what I get."

"Sex, pure and simple."

"Right. No strings attached." He rose from his chair and picked up his laptop. "I'll get back to you on what we can find on Meira. Need a lift home?"

Carmelo shook his head. "Joe's coming for me." And that made him think of Sara in the back seat of his car. He should accept JT's offer instead. But the need to punish himself for his one-eyed blindness was too great. He deserved to be reminded of her betrayal until he'd exorcised her from his mind.

"Right then. I'll talk to you tomorrow." JT pulled his keys from his pocket. "Since you've sent everyone home, would you like to take me back to the dock?"

"Yeah." The thought of being alone in his cabin with nothing but Sara's imprint on his pillow held no appeal. His phone buzzed and Joe's message came up. "Joe's on his way."

Carmelo stood, locked the cabin, and turned off the lights, his movements automated. He climbed into the motorboat beside JT, letting his friend take control on the way back to the dock. Silence lay between them; a thick, dark cloud.

They strolled up the dock to the parking lot, JT

giving Carmelo a solid yet comforting slap on his shoulder before striding in the direction of his car. "Take care, my friend. I'll be in touch as soon as I have something."

"Thanks, JT."

The purr of Carmelo's Jaguar was drowned out by the roar of JT's Ferrari engine as Joe pulled up in the car park. "Evening, sir," he greeted, stepping out of the car, and opening the rear door, his expression neutral.

Carmelo frowned, taking in the stiffness of Joe's shoulders. Joe only called him sir when he'd done something to disappoint him. Sara had an ally.

"Hey, Joe." He slid into the seat and caught the remnants of Sara's perfume as he closed the door. In the center console lay a wad of tissues and an empty tissue box. Joe hadn't cleaned the car yet.

Carmelo met Joe's glance in the rearview mirror, raising his eyebrow in a silent question. Joe was very particular about the Jaguar. It got cleaned at least once a day, sometimes twice depending on the behavior of the passengers.

"Is she okay?"

He started the car, put it into gear, and eased out onto the road before answering, "She will be."

Carmelo picked up a tube of lipstick from the floor and twirled it in his fingers before looking at the label. *Passionate Pink*. Sara's … Isadora's color. The color he'd kissed from her lips. "Car needs a clean."

"I'll clean it in good time." Joe didn't look at him as he normally would, with that friendly glance over his shoulder.

Carmelo sighed. Joe was angry with him, and that was unusual. He pocketed the lipstick. "It looks like Isadora had you wrapped around her little finger too. I made a mistake."

"That you did, Carmelo. A very stupid mistake."

"I'll let you get away with that comment, Joe. You've been in my life a long time."

Joe slowed to a stop as a set of traffic lights turned red. "It's been a very long time since we met in that dark alley, my friend. Two homeless people, cold and alone. The outcome could have been so different. Instead, we've watched each other's backs until we found our feet, and we've stuck together ever since."

"And now, Joe? Whose side are you on?"

"You know I don't take sides. But I will give you some advice. This time, think things through very carefully before you decide on what action to take. She's not a bad girl, she's only looking to do what's right."

Silence lay thick and heavy in the air all the way home. As Joe pulled up to the porch off the circular driveway, Carmelo saw the lights on inside the mansion, but knew the house would echo with emptiness. The time had come for change. The massive house would never be home to a family, so he may as well sell it and move on. A penthouse apartment might be the way to go, or he could live on the yacht. Sail wherever the tide took him.

Carmelo opened his car door and stepped out into the cool evening air. "Thank you, Joe."

His friend nodded and closed the door. "Flowers would make a good apology."

"Flowers are for break ups."

"She's not your regular type. She's a good girl."

"A good girl who planned to destroy me." Carmelo pulled on his coat to ward off the chill.

"She explained that. I believe her."

And that counted for a lot. Joe could pick a fake and a liar a mile away. "I need proof."

"You'll find it if you look in the right place."

"I'm not sure I want to look anymore, but I have JT scouting for answers anyway. Goodnight, Joe." He turned and walked towards the house where Maria stood waiting at the front door to take his coat.

"Good evening, Mr Iannello." Even she didn't meet his eyes as she usually did. "There is a fresh pot of coffee in your den. I've cleaned and pressed the new clothes Miss Stewart ... I mean, Miss de la Cruz left behind on the yacht. I thought you might want them returned to her?"

"Thank you, Maria, but no. Please donate them to charity."

Maria's brow creased in a frown, but she said

nothing other than a stilted good night and Carmelo knew he wouldn't be having her special pancakes for breakfast in the morning. She too seemed to have sided with Isadora against him.

In his den, he poured a cup of strong black coffee and flicked on the television. Settling into his chair, he watched the pit camera footage from the Daytona Beach race again, paying more attention to it this time — analyzing each pit stop, each movement, every tire change until he found what he was looking for. That moment when Isadora de la Cruz stepped from the car, ripped off her helmet and fire protection gear, glorious dark hair snaking down her back in a ponytail, and let Harlon Meira have it in a barrage of heated, angry words.

Carmelo pressed the remote to freeze the screen and studied her features. In them, he saw traces of his Sara in her lips and cheeks. Anger animated her features, her body taut with tension and her hands gesticulating wildly. Oh, she was angry, beautiful, sexy and he wanted Isadora de la Cruz as much as he'd wanted Sara — one and the same woman.

He pressed the button to go back to the start of the scene and concentrated on the recorded audio rather than the woman.

"Which bastard made changes to the suspension?"

Meira held out his hand for her helmet. "Order came from the top."

"Did you tell them it was illegal?"

"Only if you get caught."

"Which you did. What were you thinking, Harlon?"

"Money. A big, fat payday."

Carmelo wanted to smash the arrogant grin from his face, except he was long gone and in hiding somewhere in Georgia.

"And you didn't think the race officials would work it out?"

"It's a chance we took."

He stabbed the off button and watched the screen go blank. So Isadora hadn't known about the mods, but it didn't change that she thought he had or that she was prepared to lie in order to get to the truth.

His coffee had gone cold, so he placed the cup on the tray next to the pot and made his way upstairs to bed, switching off lights as he went. In his room, his bed stood cold and empty. All he wanted was her there. A need that would never be filled again.

Chapter Seventeen

Isadora tossed the sheets back, disturbing Cruzer who hissed his disapproval. "Sorry, buddy."

A quick ear scratch had him purring again, so she swung her legs over the side of the bed. The clock glowed in the dim pre-dawn light. If she got to the gym early, she'd have time to clean out her desk before Carmelo arrived for work.

Not that she had much to collect. She never left much of herself in the workplace, a habit she'd retained from traveling around the tracks with her dad. They'd never had a permanent home until now, so her carbon footprint on the environment was minimal. Working for Carmelo, it had been even more important not to leave anything lying around that might identify her. And look how well that had turned out.

The thought of him had Isadora's heart clenching

and the sharp pain of humiliation stabbing at her chest. No, she wouldn't think of the time they'd spent together. It was over now and she had a race to win. Hadn't that been the goal all along?

She showered, but each stroke of the sponge over her body reminded her of all the places Carmelo's hands had touched. So she turned up the heat and scrubbed until her skin turned pink from the effort.

An hour later, she parked her car in the basement of *Fit to Race* and let herself into the gym. Her heart skipped a beat as she recognized Carmelo's dark head bent over the screen of an exercise bike, his powerful legs pumping at the pedals, knuckles white on the handlebars. So much for coming in early in the hope of avoiding him.

For a single, stupid moment, she thought about going over to him, begging him to listen so they might work things through. After being so close to him, she hated this distance between them. She loathed that she'd hurt him. Despised that he'd hurt her.

Isadora stood, silently debating whether to leave and come back later. The muscles in his arms were pumped. No doubt he'd already completed the weight circuit. Not too long ago her hands had touched the strength of those arms. Her eyes strayed to his legs. Strong thighs and calves, contoured from exercise, Carmelo claimed a presence in a room whether in gym shorts and a t-shirt, or an Armani suit.

He slowed his speed, lifted the towel from around his neck and wiped the sweat from his face. Looking up, his gaze slammed into hers. The cyclic rhythm of his legs stilled completely as he dropped the towel back around his neck. The look of intense concentration on his face morphed into a grim mask as their eyes met and held.

Isadora's insides tumbled. She hadn't expected it to hurt so much, this distance between them. She wished she could turn back time to a place before that damned race ripped their lives to pieces. Like losing a tire on race day that left debris scattered all over the track where it got picked up by passing cars and shredded until there was little more than threads left. That's what it felt like in her heart.

Tearing her gaze away, she dropped her gym bag next to the rowing machine and went through a range of warm up stretches. It was hard to ignore his presence, but Isadora focused her energy on the routine. A good hard cardio workout would chase the ache from her chest.

Her muscles protested as she straddled the machine, pushed her feet into the stirrups and rowed until her arms screamed with the effort. She counted her breaths in time with her strokes, anything to make her forget that Carmelo was in the room.

Moving to the treadmill, she set the program to a grueling uphill routine, plugged in her earphones, and glued her gaze to the television overhead, pretending interest in the early morning breakfast show. But not even a segment on NASCAR race history could stop her eyes from straying to Carmelo and her thoughts replaying those tender scenes between them on the yacht. It seemed neither her heart nor her mind were ready to forget.

Twenty minutes later, Isadora's calf muscles demanded a break. She stopped the machine and took a quick peek at Carmelo as she dismounted. He was cooling down with some stretches. She caught his gaze in the floor-length mirrors along the east end wall and looked away quickly. She had no desire to see the contempt in his eyes that would have replaced the passion.

Regret for what she'd done churned inside her. She'd achieved what she'd set out to but the victory wasn't sweet. Instead it left a bitter taste on her tongue and an ache in her heart knowing she'd hurt him with her mistrust.

The laces on her trainers had worked loose so she bent to tie them, taking her time to secure them in a double knot. Surely he was almost done with his routine. She couldn't be in the same room with him for much longer without wanting to go over and beg him to forgive her so he could kiss her again and make this ache go away.

She glanced at the time on her wrist monitor. Not

long now before he had to be in the office. When she looked up again, he was gone.

Isadora sank from the squat onto her ass, pulled up her legs, wrapped her arms around them and let her forehead rest on her knees. Her heartbeat raced from more than the exercise. Tomorrow, she'd come later so she didn't have to see him again. The best she could do was forget his existence, no matter how badly it hurt. To forget each moment spent in his arms and the glimpse of something special between them.

Isadora stood and crossed the room to the weights section just as a personal trainer entered the gym. He looked at her and smiled, making his way over.

"Isadora de la Cruz. I'm a huge fan. My name is Mike. Mr Iannello has assigned me to your fitness program in the lead up to the race."

Her first reaction was surprise, followed closely by annoyance. Carmelo wanted his money's worth out of the Phoenix race and didn't trust her to take charge of her own fitness routine. He might know every inch of Sara, but he didn't have a clue what Isadora was capable of. Still, that wasn't Mike's problem, it was hers.

"Nice to meet you, Mike. I'm assuming you've already worked out a routine?"

They spent a few moments discussing his exercise plan, and she had to admit Mike knew his stuff. She'd be fit and ready in time for the challenges to come. Only her heart would take a lot longer to heal.

"Sounds great. Shall we start tomorrow morning?" Keen to get away, Isadora itched to clear out her desk and leave.

She'd done enough for today to kick start her journey back to being the racing professional she'd been before the scandal. And now Carmelo knew she'd be working out with Mike, surely he'd stay away from the gym during her training sessions. She wasn't sure she could focus if he didn't. But there was the part of her that wished he would show up, just so she could see him, no matter how much it hurt.

"Perfect. See you at 9 a.m.?"

Even better. Carmelo would be too busy upstairs running his business to be anywhere near the gym. "Done. See you tomorrow, Mike."

Isadora picked up her bag and headed for the shower, her mind torn between being thankful for someone behind her who would push her to the limit and being annoyed with Carmelo for not trusting her. But then she hadn't exactly given him good reason to. All she had to do now was get in and out of the office without bumping into him again.

Slipping into a pair of jeans and a button-down shirt, she stuffed her gym clothes into the bag and made her way up the stairs from the basement to the ground level elevator. She pressed the button and waited, watching the digital panel count down the floors. Thankfully, the elevator was empty. It gave her the space she needed to gather her thoughts and courage.

On the top floor, she stepped out as the doors opened and turned left down the corridor carpeted with plush grey carpet. It seemed so odd walking down there knowing it would be the last time she did so. Irrespective of her reasons for securing the job as Carmelo's assistant, she had enjoyed the challenge of working closely with him. He had an intelligent business perspective. How could she ever have believed him capable of cheating?

But the damage could not be undone. If she hadn't been so blind to Harlon's deception, things could have been so different. Except if they had been, she'd never have gotten to know the real Carmelo. The man behind the playboy image.

Opening the door to the outer office, Isadora stepped inside. Carmelo's door was closed and she let out a breath of relief. Quickly, she retrieved the few items she'd brought with her from her desk — the glass paperweight her dad had given her on her eighteenth birthday, the mug that held her pens and had traveled with her around the racetracks, and the little cosmetics bag she kept on hand for touch ups. She dropped them all into her gym bag.

Carmelo's door opened. Her heart stuttered as her hand hovered over the zipper. Closing her eyes and willing herself to stay calm, she picked the bag up and turned to face him. His eyes had no life in them, none of the light they normally held, and tiredness etched lines into his face. He hadn't slept well, judging by the dark smudges under his eyes. His shirt sleeves were rolled up and he hadn't put on a tie yet.

Isadora wanted to reach out and touch him, soothe the lines from his face, run her fingers across those tight lips and feel them soften under her hands. If only she could undo all the wrongs of the past few months.

"You left these behind." He held out his hand and in his palm lay her lipstick and the purse-sized twist-and-spray perfume spritzer she'd forgotten on the yacht.

Isadora reached out to take them, her fingers brushing his. "Thank you."

He crossed his arms over his chest and leaned against the door frame. Was he intent on standing there to make sure she didn't take anything that didn't belong to her? Had she destroyed his trust to that extreme? Not that she could blame him. Yet it didn't stop the shaft of pain that stabbed at her chest.

He kicked at the thick pile carpet with the toe of his shiny leather shoes. "There'll be a press release this afternoon announcing your reinstatement on the team. The new team manager will be in touch with you to arrange practice sessions. You've met Mike?"

"Yes." The word stuck in her throat and came out a whisper.

With a nod, he continued, "Good. He'll be traveling with you and the team to Phoenix. I expect a clean win."

It hurt that he felt he needed to remind her, that some small part of his mind still didn't believe she was innocent. "There's no other way to win."

"Remember that ... Isadora."

She hated the way her name rolled off his tongue, more of an insult than a salutation. So far removed from the loving way he'd called her Sara. His eyes were dark and unreadable, his business mask firmly in place. And every time his cold gaze raked down her body, a little piece of her died. She'd never feel the warmth of his caress again. Instead of destroying him, she'd destroyed herself.

"I have no reason to forget it."

Carmelo pushed away from the door frame and, with one last mocking look before he closed the door, said, "Good. See you in Phoenix."

Chapter Eighteen

I sadora trained harder for Phoenix than she'd trained before. Long grueling sessions both behind the wheel and in the gym, determined to give this her best shot, pushing herself beyond the point of exhaustion so she didn't have time to think about Carmelo.

He'd delivered the press release himself. It had included an apology that cleared her of all wrongdoing at Daytona Beach. That should have made her happy, instead it left her empty. She'd watched his handsome face, so perfect for the camera, and felt the weight of her heart in her stomach. She loved him but he wasn't hers anymore. He never was.

In the eight weeks leading up to the race, she'd lost weight and gained muscle strength, more than she'd ever had before, driven to chasing Carmelo from her mind. The new team were ace but that didn't keep the race marshals from inspecting their every repair or tweak closely. They were still wary with her on the team. Isadora couldn't change that, no matter how much she wanted to. The best she could do was earn back their trust and her pride.

In the back of her mind, Carmelo's parting words haunted her. *See you in Phoenix*. Just like the marshals he'd be watching too, waiting for any false moves. She was determined not to give him reason to hate or distrust her any more than he already did. Nothing could take away the yearning to have his arms around her again, even though she'd never own his heart.

Race day dawned. She'd qualified for fourth position in the knockout round by shaving three seconds off her time to finish the one-mile qualifier in 25.016 seconds. Her best time ever and the achievement trimmed some of the ache from her chest. If her dad were here, he'd be so proud and that's what she had to hold onto.

Thanks to the team the car was in mint condition, so she didn't lose points by having to use a practice car. If she had, she would have had to start the race way down the line. Score another achievement for the new Isadora de la Cruz. She'd give this race everything, give Carmelo something to be proud of one day when he looked back on this time once the bitter taste of betrayal had faded.

Mike zipped up her suit and patted her shoulder. "You've got this, Isadora. Take care out there, okay?"

He kissed her cheeks and handed her the balaclava. Mike was sweet and madly in love with his partner, Greg. They'd become good friends over the past months, rebuilding both her strength and her confidence.

Still, nerves began to curl in her belly as starting time drew nearer. Isadora swallowed against the fear that always rose in her throat pre-race, pushed away the thoughts of the danger she'd face on the track. One wrong move out there could be fatal. But once the race started and adrenaline took over, those fears and thoughts would be sucked into the vortex of race fever and forgotten.

The crew had warmed to her, enough to have a decal of her father's helmet and the dove added to the stickers next to her name on the rear fender. The harder she worked for them, the greater their trust grew, but it had been a long two months to claim the victory that came with their friendship. They surrounded her now in a flurry of wishes for good luck before settling her into the driver's seat for the final checks.

"You've got this in the bag, Isadora. Look out for that barrier on turn three."

"Stay away from the yellow line coming into the straight on turn four."

"Don't forget to hit the fuel switch in the last laps to save some of that fuel. We want to cut time off the pit stops."

"Drive it like you stole it, Isadora." This comment from the crew chief made her smile sadly. That was something her dad would say.

In her heart, she'd hoped Carmelo would be there to offer his well wishes too, but he wasn't. And she just had to deal with that no matter how much it hurt. He didn't owe her anything anymore. The lines were drawn and she had to move on.

Her spotter, Drew, did a radio check then with a thumbs up, jogged off to take up his position above the grandstand. He'd be her eyes and ears, her mirrors for the race, and she couldn't have wished for better. Things were getting real now and she pushed aside everything in her head that didn't have anything to do with the race. From here on in, it was a matter of survival.

Camera crew and sports reporters swarmed the pits, looking for pre-race interviews and gossip. Isadora was thankful her team hadn't allowed them near her. She heard via the crew that they'd interviewed Carmelo, but she'd dodged watching any of the footage, not wanting to see his reactions or the emptiness of his game face.

The drive to win chased away the pain thoughts of Carmelo always brought with them as the boys pushed her car out into the pit lane for entry into the warm-up lap. She checked the straps on her helmet and pulled on her gloves, chasing away any distracting thoughts. This whole race depended on her focus — all three hundred and twelve laps, each a mile long with thirty-six competitors on her tail and three of the best ahead of her.

The countdown started in her head and she gave the plastic dove on her dashboard a pat for luck, then her hands were ready on the steering, her body tensed for the action to come as she waited for that iconic race call, "Drivers, start your engines."

Isadora gunned the motor and let adrenaline take over as the roar of forty cars drowned out the cheers of the crowd, sending vibrations of adrenaline through her. The pace car led the procession into the warm-up laps and her foot itched to be flat on the floor the moment they moved out the way. Excitement replaced the burn of regret in her belly. There was something about the roar of a motor and the power in her hands that flicked a switch inside her soul. Race hunger, her dad had called it.

Three pace laps and the green flag would drop. She wanted out, she wanted in. Self-doubt crowded in on her. What was she doing? This was madness. She could never win this race. The thought of being more of a disappointment to Carmelo than she already was burned in her mind. Then Drew's voice sounded in her ear, giving her the lay of the field and the numbers to watch, and the butterflies in her stomach settled. This was what she knew best, her comfort zone.

The starting line approached and the green flag went down, and the time for thinking of anything other than staying in control was up. With a prayer to her dad, Isadora slipped into the bump draft with the car in front of her. By lap six, she'd found her rhythm, comfortably holding onto fourth position as the field split into packs and excitement boiled in her blood.

"Stay in the lead draft, Isadora. You have a three second lead on the second pack."

She focused on the cars in front of her and listened to Drew's commentary, ignoring the steady thump of her heart. By lap fifteen, the field had lost a couple of cars to what she was sure were spectacular crashes judging from Drew's oaths, and the pack were slaves to the yellow flag until given the all-clear. She caught a lucky break on lap twenty-five and secured third position. By lap thirty she was in the lead and barely held onto it for thirteen laps as the cars behind her vied for position. Her pulse pumped, tension burned between her shoulder blades and her fingers ached from her tight grip on the steering wheel.

"Watch your gas usage," Drew warned. "You have number five on your tail."

The race continued in a battle for the top three positions. Isadora dropped back in the field and took a late pit stop, costing her a delay of seven seconds. Her back ached, her body was coated in sweat, and fatigue had set in, making her a little teary.

Rejoining the race, she pushed her way into the lead and held on for the final fifteen laps. She didn't take it easily and that was the way she liked it.

The other drivers put up a good fight until car five touched car forty-two's rear end and sent them both into a tailspin, giving her a good lead. But soon the rest of the pack were on her ass and anticipation took flight, the taste of an upcoming victory sweet on her tongue. She hit the gas hard as the finish line approached and the checkered flag came down on her win.

Drew's cheer almost shattered Isadora's eardrums and she screamed her own satisfaction into the mike as her heart pounded through the victory lap before she eased the car back into the pit lane.

The rush of the win had her wriggling in her seat, itching to do a victory dance the moment she got out of the car. She'd won, done her father proud even if he wasn't here to share it with her. Surely she'd done Carmelo proud too?

The crew hauled her out of the car, barely giving her time to remove her helmet before sweeping her up in a flurry of hugs and pats on the back, whirling her around in circles as the adrenaline of a win peaked in the pits.

What happened next blurred in a flurry of activity and flashing cameras, champagne, and cheering. Then she held the cup in her hands and reality sunk in. She'd won the race. She'd met Carmelo's criteria. Her name was clear and she was out of a job again. The high she'd been on slammed into low gear and tears sneaked in again.

Isadora looked around for a distraction to stop them and spotted Joe. "Hey, Joe!" She waved hello and he made his way toward her.

"Well done." His smile was broad, excitement flashing in his eyes. "That was some win."

"Thanks, Joe." She accepted his warm hug and returned it enthusiastically.

"I'm sure the boss thinks so too," he assured her.

Isadora doubted that. In the far corner, Carmelo was deep in discussion with JT and the crew chief. The grim expression he wore seemed fixed in place since the day on the yacht. She'd give her heart and soul to see him the way she had before — with heat in his eyes and desire on his mind.

He left without as much as a glance in her direction. The excitement of the win, the euphoria of the battle, the sweet taste of victory leeched out of her and followed him out the door, leaving her tired and deflated.

Crew chief, Beau Morris stepped over. "Congratulations, Isadora. That was some fight you put up out there."

This would be the moment he'd ask for her suit back, the end of her career with Iannello Racing. She tapped her gloves against her thigh, fiddled with the zipper on her suit and waited for the axe to fall. Emptiness filled her heart as the fight drained out of her.

"Carmelo wants you to stay on the team for Daytona Beach. You have a job until the end of the season."

She didn't know whether to laugh or cry. Joe patted her back and kissed her cheek before leaving in the same direction Carmelo had. Around her the team cheered, hoisted her up in the air and sprayed champagne all over her. Shock numbed her mind. This should have been a victory sweeter than winning any race, but the rush of the win never came.

"We have a week to prepare. Get some rest tonight, Isadora." Beau shook her hand. "You've done the team proud. Your dad would be proud too."

The praise was high coming from a man who'd been around the tracks since she was in diapers, a man who'd championed her father through his worst days before she was old enough to know anything about racing. But her mind and body were tired. Her heart ached for the praise of the one man alive who mattered. All the praise in the world meant nothing in the wake of Carmelo's silence.

Chapter Nineteen

Carmelo's heart had been in his throat ever since Isadora took her position on the field. He'd watched each lap with his hands clenched until the blood had drained from his fingers.

Each bump draft on her rear had him clenching his teeth, waiting for the crash. Every breath he released was timed with her break from that contact. And with every lap she made it through, he knew he was hopelessly in love with the woman who'd wanted to destroy him.

Part of him had wanted her to lose the race so he didn't see her hurt in a crash. The other part laughed at his own stupidity. Three hundred and twelve laps of pure torture, as if seeing her working out in the gym and wanting her more than ever hadn't been enough.

No amount of exercise had cleared his heart or his

head. Isadora had been firmly entrenched in his mind and his body yearned for her presence in his arms. His only victory had been that he'd stopped thinking of her as Sara.

The hardest thing he'd ever done was to walk away from that race today and leave his crew chief to give her the news. He'd wanted to tell her himself, but JT had vetoed that idea. He'd said it would look like back-pedaling, especially in light of what they'd found out about Harlon Meira and the charges he was about to bring against him.

But God help him, when she came off that track all flushed and victorious, he'd wanted to hold her hard against him, feel her heartbeat and know she was alive.

Never in all the time he'd owned the team had he felt this way during a race. He'd always been mindful of the driver's safety but never in a way that had his heart stall at every close call or each turn of the track.

Carmelo poured a measure of whiskey into a glass and stepped out onto the balcony of his hotel suite to drink in the night view of Phoenix. Glittering lights stretched in all directions. At the track, they'd be shutting things down, clearing out the crowds.

And Isadora? Was she out celebrating with the team, still high on her win? He knew her room number, made sure his new assistant had booked the next best thing to the penthouse suite he now occupied. Greg was highly efficient, but nowhere near as beautiful and distracting as Isadora. He was also Mike's life partner which meant he got a running update on every minute's progress in Isadora's routine.

She'd dyed her hair back to her natural dark color, and when he'd seen her at the track, her face had been free of cosmetics. Even drawn with exhaustion, she was beautiful. For the first time today he'd got a good look at Isadora de la Cruz only to find he felt exactly the same for her as he had for the woman he'd known as Sara. It wasn't the look he'd fallen in love with, it was the woman.

The ache of loss spread through him. He missed Sara's presence around the office, her infectious laugh, her solid presence, and her warm body in his arms.

Carmelo tossed back the whiskey and walked back through the French doors into the room. On the table in his briefcase was Harlon Meira's file. Proof that he'd embezzled funds from Isadora's account to fund his gambling addiction. Evidence that he'd been the one to request the changes to the suspension of the car without input or direction from anyone else on the team. Falsified receipts, repair logs and a list of people on the take with him — it was a scandal that would rock the racing world with more force than the Daytona Beach debacle, but it would have to wait until after the final race there to be made public.

What it did was clear Isadora completely of any involvement in the whole mess. Except for her plan to expose him as a liar and a cheat. A plan that drove her to lie to him. He hated deception and disliked liars even more.

That she'd lied and misled *him* still churned the anger in Carmelo's gut. She'd used him. But then hadn't he used her too? He could understand her motive given the lengths Meira had gone to in his campaign to make her the scapegoat, to paint her as the troublemaker mistress and then take off with her life savings. Surely she hadn't lied though when she'd lain in Carmelo's arms and brought him immeasurable pleasure.

She'd get her money back. He'd make sure of that. She also deserved to know that he knew the truth. And it needed to come from him.

Carmelo picked up his key card and slipped it into the pocket of his shirt. Stepping out of the suite, he faced the elevator and pressed the button that would take him two floors down to Isadora's room.

As he walked to her door, his stomach twisted in anticipation of seeing her, hearing her voice, touching her soft skin one last time before he walked away from her for good. Another first for him. The last time he'd been this nervous was the day he and Joe had walked off the streets and asked for a job at the track. The same fear rushed through him now just as it had back then — that Isadora would refuse to see him, to talk to him.

For a moment, he leaned against the cool wall, his face resting against his forearm. From inside the room, the sound of the television filtered through the door. His heart rate increased. Straightening up, he lifted his hand, swallowed his pride, took a deep breath, and knocked.

Patience had never been his strength, so when it took a while to get an answer, irritation rose in his throat. A deep-seated need to see her kept his feet firmly planted outside her door. Then he heard the rattle of the chain and the door opened a crack.

"Carmelo."

The lack of warmth in her greeting sent a little shiver down his spine. He'd expected it, would be wise to embrace it and walk away.

"I came to apologize for not congratulating you at the track today. I had to leave." If only she knew the truth. If he'd gone anywhere near her in the pits after the race, the whole world would have seen his need for her because no way would he have been able to keep his feelings a secret. "Do you have a minute? Are you alone?"

She grimaced. "What were you expecting? An orgy? If that's what you're looking for, I'm sure a few phone calls will have your room bursting at the seams with friends in no time."

Carmelo shrugged off the barb. He deserved her disdain. "I expected an after-party to celebrate with the team at the very least."

"No parties. I'm exhausted. Three hundred-odd laps takes its toll on the mind and body. I need to rest."

"I want to talk to you."

"I can't. Not tonight. I appreciate what you've done for me, keeping me on the team, but we have nothing left to say to each other unless it's race-related."

She started to close the door. He put out his hand to stop it. "I want to know why you haven't cashed that check yet."

"I told you I didn't want your money."

"It's your money now."

Her smile was bitter. "You must really have enjoyed the sex. Thanks for the bonus. You were right, maybe I should consider prostitution my next career."

The callous words he'd thrown at her that day she'd left his yacht came back to haunt him. Oh, she had it so wrong. Not about the sex, no — because that had been mind-blowing — but about the extra half-a-million. "The money wasn't meant to buy your acceptance of my apology. I want you to buy a new future outside of this game. Please take it, Isadora."

He'd never been so confused over his feelings for a woman before. A part of him wanted her off the track, the other wanted to keep her there where he could always find her because seeing her here so soft and vulnerable, all he wanted was to hold her again. "Cash the check. Please."

She folded her arms tightly. His hands itched to reach for hers.

"Go away, Carmelo." Her voice was a quiet whisper

in the empty corridor, her gaze on the patterned carpet as she avoided looking at him.

"Look at me." When she did so reluctantly, he said, "I was proud of you out there today. You did the team proud."

She jerked her gaze away and took a step back. "You could have said that at the track. What do you want, Carmelo? You have two seconds to tell me before I close this door. And then if you don't leave, I'll call security."

Her beautiful, stubborn chin rose a notch. "Please, let me in. What I have to say won't take long. It's important." There was that too, but more than anything he wanted to reassure himself that she was okay, that she was alive and unharmed. "I've never been so scared in my life as I watched you take those turns in the race, the speed with which you hurtled down the straights, knowing that at any moment you could crash and be injured. One wrong move could have meant serious injury."

"Yet you still signed me up for Daytona Beach." Confusion chased across her face.

He wished he could see her smile again. "Not because I wanted to, but because I knew you'd want it. Now I'm not sure I could endure the torture of watching you race again."

With a sigh, she released the chain on the door, turned around and walked back into the room. Carmelo pushed the door open and followed her in, closing it firmly behind him.

Isadora sank down onto the sofa and flicked the remote to turn off the television. In the soft light of the table lamp, tiredness etched her face. She flexed her neck and rubbed at her nape.

"Headache?" He sat down next to her on the sofa.

"Yeah, along with stiff shoulders. Par for the course. I thought a hot soak in the tub and pain killers would fix some of the tension." She shrugged. "It didn't."

"Why didn't you see the team physio after the race?" He paid the man a fortune for his services and didn't regret one dime. Racing was an endurance sport and the drivers needed to be cared for. Especially Isadora. He owed her that much at least. For what he'd put her through, and for what Meira had done.

"I'll sleep it off. Say what you've come to say so I can go to bed." She arched a perfectly shaped eyebrow to remind him of his purpose in her room, but all her words did was conjure up a picture of them together in that bed, with her in his arms, safe where she belonged.

"Let me work out some of that tension for you while I talk. Your muscles will hurt tomorrow if you hold that stiffness tonight." If he couldn't hold her in his arms, at least he could ease her discomfort and the tension her body held so she could get a good night's sleep.

Isadora looked at him, her gaze wary. Carmelo shifted back on the cushions and waved a hand to the floor in front him. She hesitated, her eyes searching his, then after a moment she slipped onto the floor into the gap between his legs. She lifted the weight of her hair and twisted it into a topknot, securing it with the elastic band from around her wrist.

He shifted the robe off her shoulders and willed his mind to concentrate on forming the words he'd come to say rather than the silky feel of her skin under his hands.

"I'm about to bring criminal charges against Meira." His thumbs kneaded through the knots in her muscles, working their way towards her neck. "We found falsified receipts for repairs he never did."

"I'm not surprised. Every paycheck, he'd be down at the betting agency. I didn't realize until it was too late that he had an addiction." She winced as his hands found the pressure point on her right shoulder blade.

Under his fingers, the muscle released with a twitch. "He was also on the take. Did you know about that?" He began a gentle massage from the base of her skull out to the edge of her shoulders.

"Again, no surprise. He took most of my savings. I was lucky to be able to hold onto my apartment. Perhaps once you've finished with him, I can have a go at getting my money back. Except I know the bastard would have lost it all." She moaned as the muscle on her left shoulder released under his touch. "You missed your calling. You should have been a masseuse."

Carmelo chuckled, the sound coming out a little

huskier than planned, her pleasure fast becoming his own. A smart man would walk away, leave it be and book her in with the physiotherapist in the morning. Somewhere between seeing the exhaustion in her posture and feeling the slide of her skin under his palms, he'd lost his smarts.

"Meira's wife is ready to testify against him. She caught him cheating on her again. As soon as I lodge the case, she'll release his bank statements. The ones he didn't want her to know about."

"Another victim in his long list of gullible fools." She tipped her head back to look up at him. "I swear I didn't know he was married. No one did. He hid that secret very well, along with many others."

Lifting a hand from her shoulders, he smoothed the frown from her forehead, before continuing to manipulate the tension from her muscles. "Well, we've nailed him now. And I'll make him pay for what he did to you, to me and to the team."

Her head dropped forward, exposing the enticing curve of her neck. He yearned to press a kiss to her nape but resisted as the robe slipped further from her shoulders. From his vantage point behind her, the valley of her beautiful breasts beckoned. His body remembered those breasts well. All he needed to do was slip his hands into the front of her robe and they'd fill his palms. He no longer wanted to massage, he wanted to caress.

"Isadora ... I think I should stop now."

Carmelo's voice came out strangled. He cupped her shoulders and caressed the skin with his thumbs. She shivered under his touch. Reaching up, she released her hair from the topknot and it fell in a dark satin curtain down her back. He lifted the weight of it, let it run through his fingers and, because he had zero resistance left, he massaged the tightness from her scalp.

Her head fell back, her eyes fluttering closed and what little common sense he had left fled. Cupping her face in his palms, he leaned forward and kissed her forehead, her eyes, her nose — all sinister business at hand forgotten. Such was the power of the woman he'd known as Sara. She'd become Isadora to him now, the same person yet so much more.

She arched her neck and he kissed that too. His hands no longer obeyed the instructions his mind demanded but listened to his heart instead. He cupped her breasts in his palms, teased the nipples with his thumbs and every part of his body burned for hers.

Chapter Twenty

Isadora's bones had melted and her resistance along with them. She should stop him, tell him no, but her tongue refused to form the words and her lips preferred to be kissed.

She squirmed under the caress of Carmelo's hands, had missed his touch so much. A moan of desire left her throat before she could curb it, her need for him too great.

She sank into his touch, relished the heat of his skin against hers, and wanted to race towards a finish that would drive the doubts and fears from her mind. Anger, betrayal, lies — all faded with the sensations that grew from deep inside her and the need to feel his touch, his body, every inch of him inside her.

Carmelo lifted her off the floor and onto his lap, into his embrace. She straddled his hips, needing him with every fiber of her being, common sense a distant memory.

His hard length pressed against the apex of her thighs as he buried his head between her breasts. Her fingers raked through his hair, held him closer to the beat of her heart. Desire burned through her with each caress of his hands on her back, her hips, and thighs. The robe fell away completely and Isadora gave herself up to the sensation of his skin against hers.

It didn't seem fair that she was naked and he was fully clothed, so she eased his shirt from the waistband of his pants and slipped the buttons loose. He lifted his head, his eyes searching for signs of resistance. He wouldn't find any. She needed him tonight. They needed each other.

Isadora reached between them to release his zipper, her hands finding him, caressing his silky length until he took her face in his hands and kissed her mouth with a hunger that sent shivers all the way through her. She answered each stroke of his tongue with her own, desperate to feel every inch of his body against hers.

He shifted forward and she pushed his shirt away, keen to get her hands on the muscular contours of his body. He thrust his hips upward and she almost lost control as he wriggled until his pants were no longer a barrier.

She leaned back to look, and touch, and kiss every naked inch of him before he lifted her hips to take him in. Then his mouth was on hers again, hot and demanding. She cried out as they came together, her face buried against his neck as he filled her, all pulsing heat, and tremors of pleasure.

Exhausted, she fell against his chest, his palms soothing as he drew circles on her back. She loved the feel of him against her, the feeling of coming home in his arms. In his embrace, she was complete.

He murmured something in her ear, but she didn't quite hear the words. Tiredness washed over her in waves, the rush of what they'd shared stealing the last of the adrenaline from her system. Then he was moving under her, standing, carrying her in those big, beautiful arms and laying her down on the cool sheets.

She tightened her grip on his neck, dragging him down with her. "Stay with me."

"I'm not going anywhere." He climbed into bed beside her and drew the covers up over them, spooning her into the curve of his body.

With his warmth at her back and his breathing steady in her ear, she slept.

In the dim light of dawn, his lips found her skin again, his hand drew circles on her belly, reaching lower to cup the part of her already willing. She pressed her body back into his, feeling him hard, long, and ready.

She placed her hand over his where his fingers

worked an incredible magic that had every muscle clenching with expectation.

"Good morning, Isadora," he whispered against the shell of her ear, his tongue tracing the shape.

She turned in his arms, lay flat on her back and raised a hand to cup his face. "Good morning." She searched his face. Whatever happened between them after Daytona Beach, she'd have no regrets about last night.

His head came down and lips touched hers in a soft, gentle caress that was more exciting than the hunger with which he'd kissed her last night. This wasn't just sex. This was making love. The look in his eyes softened. Her lids fluttered closed so she could hold on to that moment. Then his hands were on the move, stroking, cupping, making sweet magic on her skin.

His fingers pressed against her, entered the slick warmth where her muscles clenched around them. Her hand slipped from his face, down his neck to his chest where the strength of his heart beat under her palm.

She followed the trail from his breastbone down to his navel where she encountered the silky tip of his erection. Her fingers played across it, his indrawn breath bringing a smile of satisfaction to her lips then she wrapped her hand around his length and caressed every inch of him.

"You drive me crazy." The heat in his gaze paid testimony to that.

She matched each tease of his fingers inside her with a stroke of her own, her eyes on his until with a groan of frustration, he took her mouth. Each dip of his tongue and nip of his teeth drove her body to frenzied new heights, then the time for teasing was over.

He pushed himself up and settled his weight into the cradle of her hips. Gripping her ass, he plunged into her as she wrapped her legs around his waist to take each fevered stroke.

Later, she lay in his arms, curled up against his side, her head on his chest and his thumb caressing her shoulder. He'd come to talk and they hadn't done much of that. Who knew what would happen after Daytona Beach? Isadora wasn't even sure what they had between them or if it would last. All that mattered was he wasn't angry anymore, that he'd found out the truth and that her actions had been justified.

Chapter Twenty-One

The week flew by in rush of travel, training, and preparation for Daytona Beach. Isadora wasn't entirely sure what had resulted from their hook up in Phoenix, but other than a bouquet of roses arriving in her room after he'd left, she hadn't seen or heard from Carmelo.

It was just as well she hadn't. She couldn't afford anymore distractions. Not with four hundred miles of track and two hundred and sixty-seven laps looming. Still, her gut remained unsettled and unease filled her mind. How could he switch what they had between them on and off so easily?

"Come on, Isadora, put some effort into it. What's the matter with you?" Mike stilled the swing of the boxing bag.

"Sorry."

She tried harder to focus on her training, the makeshift track gym, and Mike's instruction but couldn't shake the feeling that something awful was about to happen. Isadora had never been big on premonitions before a race, so she couldn't blame superstition. Perhaps the whole mess with Harlon was about to blow up again if Carmelo did decide to bring charges against him. Or maybe it was Aylesha's warning that day in San Francisco to watch her back that had her on edge. Thankfully, she hadn't shown up in Phoenix. Daytona Beach, however, might be different.

"Look, let's call it quits, okay?" Mike pulled off his gloves. "You're the fittest you'll ever be, but you need to keep your mind on the game."

Isadora agreed. It wouldn't help to clutter her thoughts with maybes. "Yeah, I know."

"Okay, go get some rest. Race start is at 6.30p.m. Don't forget to do your warm-ups before getting into the seat."

She sighed and hugged Mike. "I won't forget. Will you be there?"

"Wouldn't miss it for the world. You're gonna ace it."

She'd give it her best shot. All she needed to do was get Carmelo out of her head. Digging in her gym bag for a towel, the light flashing on her phone caught her eye, indicating a message. Isadora picked it up, swiped to unlock the screen and tapped on the message icon.

Good luck for tonight. Stay safe. C.

Her heart fluttered. He hadn't forgotten her. Nothing good could come of it. After Daytona Beach, she'd be out of his life. Carmelo didn't do happy ever after. And even though they'd cleared the air on the subject of Daytona Beach, there'd always be a little doubt in their minds.

Thanks xx. She messaged him back.

What else was there to say? She wanted to ask if he'd be there watching, if he'd come to the party that would end the season for the year. If he'd dance with her then take her home and make love to her again like he had in Phoenix. But dreams were for Sara Stewart. Isadora de la Cruz could only afford reality.

Rest was impossible. She paced the dirt outside the team's RV, a bottle of water for hydration. She should be lying down on one of the bunks inside, but her feet needed to run off some of the pent-up energy that churned inside her.

She hitched up her track pants, tied the string a little tighter and started a slow-paced jog down Motor Home Row where the line of RVs housed some of the drivers. Unlike them, she didn't have one of her own and sharing with the pit crew wasn't a great idea for a girl on her own. Not that she didn't trust any of them, it was more that they cared about her reputation which is why she was given a room at the nearest hotel.

As she increased her pace and measured her

breathing, her mind worked over the line up, the competitors, her place on the track. The pit crew were doing the final tune ups, checking the safety gear, her helmet, and HANS device — all the things pertinent to saving her life in a crash. Still that didn't settle the unease that dogged her mind.

She had no intention of crashing, only winning and taking home the final cup for the season, for the Iannello Race Team, and then her dream would be over unless she could find another team prepared to gamble on Isadora de la Cruz.

She finished her lap of the park and spent a few moments doing stretches to cool down before moving toward the pits and her crew to take in the pre-race discussions and predictions.

The closer the time came to the race, the edgier she felt. Isadora flexed her fingers, rotated her wrists, and rolled the tension from her neck and shoulders. It refused to budge and she wished Carmelo was there to ease it away.

The memory of what had happened after the last massage he'd given her warmed her cheeks. She stamped her feet in the dirt to dispel the heat that flowed through her at the thought. She needed to concentrate on the competition not on the man who made her heart race.

"Relax. We've got this in the bag." Her spotter,

Drew, patted her shoulder. "Follow my lead and I'll have you taking a gap and catching a side draft in no time."

"Cheers, Drew." She high-fived the hand he held up and wished she had his faith.

Isadora thought of the three and a half million-dollar check Carmelo had handed her. It still sat tucked away in the envelope in a safety deposit box at her bank. And that's where it would stay. She had no intention of cashing in on Carmelo's gesture, even though he'd begged her to. When the season was over and he sent her away again, she'd hand the check back to him. Then she'd turn the page and move on to whatever came next. A future that stretched ahead of her an empty void.

The crew chief came to find her for the practice laps and she went through the paces on auto pilot, anticipating the turns, warming the tires, looking for the hot spots on the track, studying her competitors and their driving styles, all while trying to dispel that niggling feeling that had taken up residence in her tummy.

Joe turned up as the crew pushed her back into the garage for the final checks before race start.

"Hey, Isadora." Joe held out a single red rose as she climbed out of the car.

"Thanks, Joe. Lovely to see you here. Got tired of watching it on television?"

"I'm here with Mr Iannello, but I'm glad to be able to

see it for real. I wouldn't miss it for the world. You go get 'em, Tiger."

Carmelo was here. Her heart pounded and she couldn't stop the smile that slipped onto her lips. Even if this was goodbye, she'd at least get to see him one last time.

"Well, I'm glad you're here, Joe."

He leaned in to hug her. "Good luck and you be careful out there, okay?"

"I promise I will."

She couldn't stay the hope that Carmelo would show up in the pits too, but when the time came to line up on the track, there was still no sign of him. Isadora ignored the stab of regret and focused on the chief's instructions instead. Then she attached her helmet and HANS, climbed into the car, and strapped into the six-way harness, pushing all thoughts of Carmelo and the hot steamy nights in his bed aside.

The safety tech checked the clasps on her harness, the straps on her helmet connecting to the HANS device and handed her a pair of driving gloves. In her ear, Drew tested the radio connection and she listened to the responses from the rest of the crew before she gave him hers. Her stomach churned in anticipation as they started to push her out into pit lane.

This was it. Her final ride for Iannello Racing, the end to a chapter in her life — the thought brought a cold hand to her heart and sadness to her throat. She didn't want it to end. She wanted to turn back the clock to the hotel room, tell Carmelo she loved him, beg him to stay with her and never let her go. But perhaps that interlude in her room had been his way of saying goodbye.

Isadora flexed her fingers on the steering wheel. By the end of the race, they'd be stiff enough to need to be pried off. The flag went up and the call came, "Drivers, start your engines." The rush of adrenaline that was part of every race start shot through her blood as she lined up in position behind the pace car.

A sense of *de ja vu* settled over her, the race start in Phoenix a not-too-distant memory. She prayed that this race would be as uneventful as Phoenix had been. Although there'd been a few crashes, there'd been no major incidents. Surely that had to be a good omen, right?

The pace car drifted out into pit lane signaling the start of the first lap.

"And the race is on!" shouted Drew.

Isadora caught a bump draft first up, just as she had in Phoenix, then maintained a steady pace for the next twenty-five laps, carefully taking instruction from Drew. She had this in the bag.

A few rookies squeezed past her and shot through. She let them. Skill always won over hot-headedness. She smiled as Drew confirmed the rookies had nudged and spun out, leaving her holding steadily onto fifth.

She cruised for another three hundred and fifty laps,

maintaining points and position with a steady pattern. They'd lost half the pack behind her, according to Drew, in some spectacular crashes. This was too easy. The unease tipped back into her mind as she flexed her neck to ease the muscles as much as the HANS device would allow.

"Okay, Isadora. Number three in the leader's bump draft. You've got a clear lane to the right into turn three."

She focused on the tail of the car in front of her as brake lights illuminated and took the move to the right. Isadora fought with the wheel to control the upward slide, her heart pounding with the effort to keep the car away from the barrier, then gunned it into the gap.

"Take it into car nine's side draft. Watch your drift in the turn."

Turn three approached fast, the pack ahead tight as they prepared for it. She tightened her grip to prepare for the momentum that would take her around the bend. The smallest error, her own or someone else's, could have her crashing into the wall. Her jaw clenched as she focused on the turn, her stomach churning with excitement or trepidation, she no longer knew which.

In her ear, Drew yelled, "What in God damn hell is that idiot doing?" and her heart stalled for a split second. She shook off the fear that curled up her spine.

"What?" She was seconds from taking the turn. Now

would be a good time for Drew to warn her if there was something happening up ahead.

"Number twenty-three is making a run for it from the back. There's nowhere for him to go. He's not slowing down."

That meant he was on her tail and if she didn't make the corner it could get ugly. Isadora focused on taking that corner, her mind blocking out the panic in Drew's voice, and the sick, sinking feeling in her gut.

Contact came hard and fast, a bone shuddering slam that forced her body forward, her harness pushing her back. Sparks flew as the right-hand side of the car connected with the barrier, throwing her sideways in the seat. Then her world spun out of control as another car T-boned her side to send her spinning, a dizzying vortex of light, debris, and smoke.

She closed her eyes against it, tried not to swallow the thick black taste of burning rubber, knowing that to try and control the spin was futile. She just had to hold on and pray she didn't get hit again.

When people said they'd seen their life flash before their eyes, she'd never believed it. She did now. Her body followed the vortex of the spin, her insides tumbling like the contents of a blender, nausea rising. She'd be lucky to escape this without internal injuries. If she escaped it all.

"Isadora! Oh sweet Mother Mary and Joseph. Isadora!"

She had no breath left in her lungs to answer Drew. She heard him yelling at the other spotters, his words a jumble of oaths and questions. Disoriented as inertia held her captive, the other car seemed to come out of nowhere, slamming into what was left of hers. Airborne, the force threw her against the restraints. The deafening roar of tearing metal screeched across her eardrums. Unbearable pain stabbed her chest, arms, and legs. She tumbled over and over, coming to earth with a sickening thud, her world topsy turvy, a surreal scene of debris scattering away from the body of her car in slow motion. The front end of her car separated from the body and skidded across the grass. She screamed out to Carmelo, the sound forced from her tight throat, then silence screamed inside her head as her world crashed.

Chapter Twenty-Two

"Oh my God!" The commentator shouted his disbelief as Carmelo watched the carnage unfold on the screen from the pit garage. "In a shock move, car number twenty-three has come up from the rear of the pack and rear-ended Isadora de la Cruz in number eight. This is a disaster, folks."

He could only stare in horror as her spotter swore over the radio, his heart in his throat.

Isadora's car hit the wall in turn three then slammed back onto the wheels in a bone-jarring move only to be T-boned by another out of control victim of the multi-car crash that resulted in the track being strewn with flying debris.

Ice cold fingers of fear crept up his spine as he gripped the back of a chair in the pit garage. He hadn't seen her before the race. He should have come down sooner. He shouldn't have let her drive. If anything happened to Isadora …

The impact sent the wreck into an uncontrolled spin. Number twenty-three came for her again, the force rocketing the car into the air and sending it tumbling back down on the roof. Carmelo's own body jerked against the impact. He closed his eyes against the scene, but the horror continued to unfold in his memory, so he forced them open again. Pain, sharp and fierce, stabbed at his heart as he watched helplessly, his feet immobilized on the cold concrete floor, shock numbing his legs.

Sparks lit the track as the back of the pack tried to avoid the carnage and failed, while what was left of Isadora's car slid to a halt on the grass.

His heartbeat thundered, a sickening feeling taking hold of his gut as flames leaped from the rear. *Oh sweet Jesus, no.* His instinct was to run out there, but as he turned to do so, the crew chief placed a hand on his arm to stop him.

"Wait, Carmelo. If you go out there now, security will only stop you. Let the response crew do their job."

He ran a hand through his hair, frustration biting his ass. He had to get to Isadora.

"The safety team are out. And there's the red flag." The commentators' box erupted in furor. "The red flag is up. The Daytona 500 has been shut down. There is a massive pileup on the track, folks. This is bad, really bad. We haven't seen anything like this since 2001 when we lost a driver. What was number twenty-three thinking?"

Carmelo's fingers clenched as the flames were extinguished and the emergency crew went in to drag Isadora from the car. The cameras zoomed in on the wreck, upside down on the grass. The car had done what it was designed to do and the front end had sheared off ensuring Isadora couldn't be crushed by the weight of the engine.

"I need to get out there! I need to see her!" His voice broke over the words as he shook the chief's hand from his arm.

"There's nothing you can do for her." Beau's words were stern. "You'll just be in the way. She'll be fine. We have the best safety gear in that car, and the paramedics are right there with her. Let them do their job."

He knew somewhere in the back of his mind that Beau was right, but the need to see it for himself forced him to pace the floor while he waited, his attention continuously drawn to the drama unfolding on the screen.

"This is not looking good, folks."

A crew member tore back the black window webbing that prevented the driver's limbs from being exposed during a crash. They were having difficulty getting her out of the mangled mess.

Carmelo ran a hand over his face, pressed it to his lips to stop the nausea from rising. His mind numbed; his vision blurred. Every moment they struggled, spelled disaster for Isadora. Beside him the pit crew watched, a terrible silence descending in the garage.

They dragged her from the car, a limp rag doll, and the paramedics were on her in an instant. He'd never cried a tear in his life, not even as a boy on the streets with hunger churning in his gut and danger snapping at his heels, but now his eyes burned with the effort to hold the tears back. His head thumped in tune with his heart.

The crew around her made it difficult to see what was happening. He could do nothing but wait it out with the frustration eating at him for being held back and able to do nothing. *Please God let her be alive*. If she wasn't ... no, he didn't want to think about that. She had to live. He loved her.

"They have her out, but she's not moving." The commentator's words fell into the silence, a loud sonic boom in the room. Carmelo smashed his fist into the wall, despair eating away at him. A hand came down on his shoulder. Joe.

"Take it easy."

Carmelo held his breath and waited for the thumbs up signal that would indicate she was okay. When it didn't come, he had to remind himself to breathe as numbness seeped through him.

He tried to distract the dark thoughts by watching the tow trucks clearing the wrecks and the cleanup crew picking up debris off the track, but his eyes were drawn back to the carnage and Isadora's lifeless body.

Then, as he was about to give up hope, the signal went up along with a roaring cheer from the crowd. She wasn't getting up but she was alive. Relief flooded him with dizzying speed. She was alive, it was a start.

"Word from the field is that Isadora de la Cruz was knocked unconscious during the crash. She is responding, but she's pretty beat up. Team Iannello is big on safety features in their cars which is lucky for Ms. de la Cruz. Without her HANS device, she could have suffered horrific neck and spinal injuries. The question on everyone's lips is … what was number twenty-three's driver doing?"

Carmelo didn't give a flying dime what the driver of car twenty-three was doing, he wanted the man to pay for almost killing Isadora. He tuned out of the commentary as they lifted her onto the stretcher. Watching them load her into the back of the ambulance, his chest tightened and his throat constricted, the fear of the unknown gripping his heart and stomach.

"I want that driver's ass in a sling, Joe. JT better find out what the hell happened out there."

"I bet he's already on it." Joe's hand rested on Carmelo's arm. "Come, I have a car out front. If we leave now, we'll be at the hospital's ER department when the ambulance arrives."

Carmelo tore his concentration from the screen. Around him the team murmured amongst themselves, shock reverberating around the garage. The crew chief demanded answers from Isadora's spotter but the words all mingled together in his head, creating a buzz instead of making sense.

He dialed JT's number as he hurried to the car alongside Joe, hollow inside.

"I saw it." JT didn't waste time on greetings. "I'll be there as soon as I can get on a flight."

"Find out what the idiot in car twenty-three was up to." Numbness gave way to anger. "I want his balls on the chopping block."

"Already on it. And Carmelo?"

"Yeah?"

"For what it's worth, buddy, I'm sorry. I hope she makes it."

He couldn't imagine life without her if she didn't. Carmelo hung up and climbed into the car next to Joe for the longest seven-minute ride of his life.

They arrived seconds before the ambulance did when Isadora was rushed through the doors. He caught a glimpse of her pale face, her neck in a brace, before they swept past him, wasting no time in getting her seen to.

He wanted to stop them, to see her, to talk to her, to tell her he loved her, but time was critical and any delays would be the difference between life and death. So he had no choice but to wait.

Joe brought him a foam cup filled with foul-tasting coffee the consistency of mud but turning the cup in his hands gave him something to do while they waited. He filled out forms with what little information he had about her.

Hospital administration didn't care that she liked shrimp or picnics on Angel Island, or a glass of Napa Valley Chardonnay. They wanted to know about allergies and previous injuries. It made him realize how little he knew about Isadora Sara Stewart de la Cruz, especially when he had to put his name down as next of kin.

The hours ticked by slowly and the visitors' lounge filled up with pit crew. Outside the hospital, the press waited for news. JT had boarded a flight and was searching for answers on the rogue driver's attack on Sara. And Carmelo waited. For something, for anything. It felt like forever before a surgeon entered the lounge and took him aside.

"I'll start with the good news. She's going to be okay."

The blood drained from his head in a rush, leaving him dizzy with relief. "But?" There was always a 'but'.

"She has a ruptured L1 vertebrae, a fractured tail bone and substantial bruising to the chest and ribs. Her leg is broken in two places —mid-shaft tibia and fibula — and she has a broken arm, a fractured wrist, and a dislocated shoulder. She's taken a good shaking, but thankfully there are no internal injuries and no bleeding. The CT scan showed no long-term damage although she does have mild concussion with a small amount of swelling that should recede quickly. Ms. de la Cruz is a lucky girl."

Carmelo rubbed a hand over his face, exhaustion edging its way into his body. It must be way past midnight, but the need to sleep had faded leaving only bone-deep weariness seeping in. "Can I see her?"

The surgeon nodded. "Only for a little while though. She's in a lot of pain. We're taking it easy on the meds for a few hours until we can be sure there are no side effects from the concussion. We've set the bones we can, but we'll have to operate on the leg tomorrow. She'll need screws and a brace. It's going to be a long road to recovery."

He swallowed the bile that rose in his throat. Isadora would make a full recovery. He'd make sure of it. "Thank you."

Carmelo shook the doctor's hand and followed him into the room where Isadora lay, her broken arm in a cast, suspended in the air. Her leg too was elevated at an angle, her toes discolored with deep bruising at the end of the bulky bandage.

His heart contracted at the sight of her beautiful face, so pale and drawn. Her eyes were closed, the lashes sweeping her cheeks. He smoothed her hair back from her forehead. She'd have some bruising on her face from the impact of the helmet against the headrest restraint, but it would be minimal. They'd put tubes in her nose for oxygen because her chest injuries made breathing difficult. Her eyes fluttered open.

"Hey," he said, kissing the blue-black blemish on her forehead.

"Hey." Her voice was barely a whisper above the beep of the machine monitoring her vital signs.

"You didn't have to go to this extreme to get my attention, you know. A phone call would have done it," he teased to cover up the breath that hitched in his throat as the reality of how close he'd come to losing her began to sink in.

Her lips twitched a little. He stroked her swollen fingers where they protruded from the cast. They were cold under his touch so he held them between his palms, careful not to jar her wrist.

"You scared the shit out of me." Carmelo sat down in the chair next to the bed and talked because if he didn't, he'd make a fool of himself and cry. "The crew are waiting in the visitors' lounge. They send their best wishes. I think you shaved a few years off Drew's life. Mike's and Joe's too. JT's asking questions about what happened out there. I'll get answers, I promise."

She tried to say something, but he pressed a finger to

her lips. "No, don't say anything. Rest and get better, baby."

His gaze moved to the IV bag and the steady drip of fluid down the tube. Anything she wanted she'd have. Because as he sat there holding her fingers in his hand, it hit him that he was the reason she was here in this mess.

If he'd let her go after Phoenix, she wouldn't be lying here all battered, broken, and bruised. If he hadn't slept with her, he wouldn't have wanted to keep her with him for as long as he could. And if he hadn't employed Harlon Meira, she wouldn't be in his life at all.

Carmelo's phone beeped and he released her fingers to check the message from JT.

Harlon Meira paid a driver to switch places so he could push Isadora's car out of the race.

Jesus! Carmelo's heart skipped a beat as his gaze flew to Isadora's face. He could have killed her. What kind of a bastard had he hired to get the team into this mess?

And what a sad judge of character he'd been. The man had him fooled with his exceptional references and track record. A record Carmelo now realized Meira had paid someone to create for him. And by going after him, putting the pressure on him for a confession on the Daytona Beach race modifications, Carmelo had made Isadora a target for revenge.

His phone rang and JT's number came up again. He

tapped the screen to answer and held the phone to his ear. "JT?"

"I've just had a call from Aylesha. She's hysterical. She told Meira about you and Isadora hooking up at the party on the yacht, and he didn't take kindly to the news. Seems he doesn't want her but he doesn't want anyone else to have her either. He's not happy that she's mixed up with you. He told Aylesha he'd kill Isadora, but she didn't take it seriously. She thought he was blowing smoke out his ass so when he asked for it, she gave him the race line up for Daytona Beach."

Carmelo's heart jumped to his throat. "Then he paid off some rookie to step down so he could ram her off the track. Why the hell would Aylesha do something so stupid?"

"She had her own little vendetta against Isadora de la Cruz as one of the many women in Meira's life. She warned him that Isadora was doing some digging of her own and that you knew it was him who fixed that race, that we were coming after him with criminal charges. I'm sorry, Carmelo. I didn't think she was paying any attention to our discussions. It's over, of course. I can't trust her ever again, but she'll co-operate with the investigation. I'm about to give a full report to the police which is bound to make our friend Meira very nervous when they come knocking on his door."

"Nervous enough to run?"

"Nervous enough to come after you."

Guilt gnawed at his gut. He looked back at the woman he'd fallen in love with. She'd slipped into sleep, the even beep of the monitor on her heart a reminder of the damage he'd done. He'd put her in Meira's path of destruction, almost got her killed. If Meira had Carmelo in his sights, he wouldn't hesitate to hurt them both. If she wasn't associated with Carmelo in any way, maybe Meira would leave her alone. He had to let her go, for her own safety.

"Let him come. As long as he never touches Isadora again."

"We'll make sure he doesn't."

Chapter Twenty-Three

The walls of her hospital room closed in around her, a private hell she'd existed in for ten long, painful days. Under the casts on her arms, Isadora's skin itched like crazy and she couldn't do a damn thing about it. Mike teased her, waving the knitting needle in front of her face.

"If you don't stop being a grump, I won't scratch that itch for you."

Mike and his knitting needle had become her best friends. The wire cage around her leg made sleeping, sitting, and lying down uncomfortable and she wasn't allowed to walk on it yet which meant she was pretty much stuck in bed or a wheelchair, being driven stir crazy.

Her ribs were on the mend, as was the bruising to her chest, but her whole body was still a kaleidoscope of color ranging from yellow to black. Black like her mood.

"Scratch it, or so help me God as soon as I'm able, I'm going to hide your *Dirty Dancing* DVD."

Mike sighed. "No one takes Johnny Castle from me." He inserted the knitting needle into the cast and gave her skin a couple of soothing scratches. "Better now?"

Isadora closed her eyes with relief. "Yes, thank you."

"So ..." Mike knew how to draw out the word with perfect dramatic effect. "Seen the sexy Carmelo lately?"

"No." She hadn't seen him since the morning after the accident when she'd woken up to find him sleeping in the chair next to her bed, his feet up next to hers and a hospital blanket thrown carelessly across his chest. Ten days, four hours and twenty-nine minutes ago.

Mike's eyebrow shot up in surprise. "He took it hard."

"He would. It cost him money. The car was totaled."

"He wasn't worried about the car, Isadora."

"Then where is he?"

There'd been flowers and get well soon cards from the team, but nothing from him. Now it seemed she was destined to sixteen weeks of recovery and rehabilitation to fix her body when her heart was beyond repair.

She didn't understand how he could blow hot and cold like he did. But then she didn't understand anything anymore. When Drew had told her how Harlon had run her off the track, she'd thought it was some kind of joke. Until JT Horne confirmed it.

Mike tapped the knitting needle against her cast. "Pay attention to these lips." He pointed to his mouth. "Greg says Sexy Carmelo is a grumpy bear around the office since he got back. And Greg should know being his new assistant and all."

Isadora rolled her eyes, wincing a little because of the tenderness of a post-concussion headache behind them.

"I'm sure Greg is a grumpy bear too since you're here babysitting me instead of keeping him warm at night. That might be rubbing off on the boss."

"I think it's because Carmelo's in love with you. Think about it — your own personal trainer ... i.e. *moi* ... all your bills paid for this fancy private hospital room, all your medical bills paid, and his own lawyer at your disposal to ensure Harlon Meira not only goes down, but never gets up again. He even has his chauffeur taking care of your plants and your cat."

"I think you're a hopeless romantic. He's doing all that because he feels responsible. I'm an employee, and Carmelo takes good care of his employees. If he's in love with me, why isn't he here scratching my itch?" She held up her left hand so Mike could administer relief to the skin on her fractured wrist instead of using the knitting needle as a drumstick.

Mike's grin turned downright cheeky. "Who says he isn't? And if you ask me, he's already well and truly scratched your itch. He'd be mad if he didn't."

Isadora laughed then groaned because it hurt. "You're the only person in the world I'd let get away with a comment like that. You've kept me sane with your cheeky sense of humor this past week. And while I'd rather it was Carmelo holding my hand through the battery of tests and examinations, I am truly grateful to have a true friend beside me." She hadn't realized how lonely she'd been on her own. How lonely she'd be again when this was all over.

Mike wiped the knitting needle down with an anti-bacterial wipe. "Well, I think it's true that he's in love with you and so does Greg." He looked at his watch. "And that's why he's about to walk through that door right about ... now."

There was a tap at the door and it opened. Carmelo came in followed closely by JT.

Mike cocked an eyebrow. "See, I told you so."

Her heart did a little dance and she was glad they'd removed the device that monitored it or she wouldn't have been able to hide the effect seeing Carmelo again had on her. He looked tired and drawn. Greg was right. He even looked a little grumpy.

What he didn't resemble was a man in love. She was sure Mike had that wrong. If he did love her, why was he playing this game of advance and retreat?

Mike stood. "Carmelo, JT," he greeted them. "I'll be back later, Isadora. Anything you want me to bring back?"

She shook her head. "No, thank you."

With a wave, he was gone, leaving her alone with the two men.

"Feeling any better?" JT asked.

Ever since he'd found out Aylesha was partly responsible for her crash, JT had been very nice to her. Perhaps that was due to the fact Carmelo was paying his fee in her case against Harlon.

"Yes, thank you. I'll feel even better once they let me take a real shower." Sponge baths were just not what they were cracked up to be. Isadora longed for a long, hot bath or shower, but that privilege was at least another few weeks away when her casts came off. And even then she'd still be hampered by the contraption on her leg.

She looked over JT's shoulder at Carmelo and caught his gaze. His nod of greeting didn't make the cut when all she wanted was his arms around her and his voice in her ear telling her everything between them would be all right.

"Your surgeon thinks you're well enough to go home soon. We've liaised with a surgeon in San Francisco who will take over your case and monitor your progress. You'll have a private nurse to take care of you until your casts come off."

It all sounded so cold and calculated. JT Horne was taking no chances. While she was grateful that she'd have help when she got home and during rehabilitation, none of it mattered if she'd lost Carmelo.

Isadora picked at the blanket over her legs, her fingers restricted by the heavy casts. At least the swelling had gone down a little and her fingers no longer resembled fat, purple sausages.

"Isadora?" JT prompted her out of her thoughts.

"Of course, thank you."

She'd never been more confused in her life. Surely if Carmelo cared enough to arrange for her to be looked after, he cared about her? He'd spent the night at her bedside after the accident, for God's sake. That had to mean something. Why then was he leaving all these decisions up to his lawyer and standing in his shadow not saying a word?

Hurt rose to the surface. She should have expected it. She knew the rules of playing the game with men like him. She was damaged goods. Her legs and arms would always bear the unattractive, less than perfect scars of the accident. She was no longer someone to be seen on the arm of San Francisco's most eligible bachelor. She never had been. Thoughts crashed through her head, muddled by the strength of the painkillers, sabotaged by post-trauma emotions.

There'd always been a time limit, a use by date, on their affair — she could hardly call it a relationship. The rules had always been clear and there was no reason that what they'd had between them could be any different to what JT and Aylesha had — a mutually beneficial agreement. Only Isadora had wanted more.

"Carmelo tells me you haven't cashed your check yet."

She looked over at Carmelo again, who studied his shoes with feigned interest, and Isadora wondered why he couldn't just ask her himself. "No." Her reasons for it would remain her own until she re-addressed that envelope back to its rightful owner.

JT raised his eyebrows at her snappy tone. "Okay. Well, I guess things have been a little busy lately."

"No shit." Surliness replaced the snap and she realized Mike was spot on. She was grumpy. But surely she had every right to be. She was the one held together by screws and plaster casts.

Carmelo's gaze finally met hers, his eyes dark and pensive, his beautiful mouth drawn in a grim line. He raked a hand through his hair and then drew it down over his face and the day-old growth of beard. She could tell from the tension in his shoulders, he was holding back. He had something to say, but he wasn't saying it.

Isadora wished JT would leave them alone so that her anger could spill over and whatever frustration Carmelo was holding would be released. She wanted a showdown not this terrible silence she didn't understand.

"Right, well ..."

JT shifted uneasily as the tension in the room grew to snapping point. There was some satisfaction in seeing Mr Cool-and-Calm rattled, but it wasn't him she was in love with or had been hurt by.

"So, we have a few things we need to wrap up at the track with the race officials and that will take a couple of days. By then, you should be ready for release and we'll take you home with us on the jet. It will be a lot more comfortable for you than a commercial airline."

"I don't need an escort home. I'll find my own way and pay my own fare to get there." Bitterness edged into her tone. "You have no need to worry. I don't want any more money. I'm not after compensation for what happened at the track. And what happened between Carmelo and I will be our dirty secret with no repercussions."

"That's not what this is about, Isadora. We're genuinely invested in your full recovery." JT's voice was calm and quiet, but all it served to do was make her angrier.

Perhaps it was a combination of what had taken place since Daytona Beach, her love for Carmelo that would go unfulfilled and a large amount of disgust for her own gullibility, but she let everything boil over.

"You're invested in maintaining an image — both of you. You were so quick to pay me off with a check for what happened on the yacht in San Francisco, then showed the world how generous you were by letting me keep my job after Phoenix and now that's turned sour, you're sweeping the damage under the carpet by taking good care of me." As the bitter words left her lips, pain clenched her heart because they sounded so believable to her ears.

"You know that's not true."

JT tried to reason with her, but Carmelo remained quiet, his gaze fixed on a point over her head, his face unreadable, his mouth closed against any denial.

"Get out." Soul-searing pain bubbled up in her chest, far worse than the injuries she'd sustained in the crash. "Go."

As they turned and left, the tears burning behind her eyes fell and she cried with sobs that shook her battered body. The pain didn't hurt nearly as much as Carmelo's silence.

Chapter Twenty-Four

Carmelo welcomed the winter chill that seared his skin, reached in, and froze the pain he'd felt since he'd walked out of Isadora's hospital room in Daytona Beach and returned home to San Francisco. He reassured himself it was for the best. Let her think the worst of him. He deserved it.

The view of the Bay from the pilot house was gray, a miserable, stormy color that reflected his mood. It was as if a piece of him had died on that track when Isadora's car had crashed and she'd lain in that bed, all battered and bruised, scarred for life because of him. Guilt was a cold bedfellow.

"I thought you hated liars." JT passed him a glass containing a double measure of whiskey.

He took it and raised an eyebrow. "Meaning?"

"When will you tell Isadora the truth?"

He didn't want to talk about Isadora, but then he didn't want to think about her either and look how that was working out. "I don't need to."

JT swirled the whiskey around in his glass, checking the color before taking a sip. "So you're going to go through the rest of your life being a miserable asshole, letting her think you tried to pay her off."

Carmelo shrugged. "That's what I did, isn't it?"

And ever since he had, he'd been right back in that funk he'd started out in the day he'd invited Isadora onto the yacht for Tony's party. A lifetime ago. The house had stood empty ever since. He hadn't been able to go back to the silence. He'd asked Joe to have the realtors value it for the market. He wanted to be here, on the yacht in the Bay, with the stormy waters and the miserable weather, where everything in his cabin reminded him of Isadora and the mistakes he'd made.

"Mike tells me she's doing well. Her leg is almost healed and if the surgeon is right, she'll walk without a limp."

"I know. Greg has been updating me."

His assistant had a soft spot for Isadora. If Greg wasn't so in love with Mike, Carmelo might be worried. He let a grim smile tug at his lips. Greg had also been hounding him to check on her.

"You should call her." JT put his glass down on the table. He pointed to Carmelo's phone. "Now."

"No point."

JT sighed. "Fine. Suit yourself. What are you doing about *Fit to Race* and the clothing range? You'll have to make a decision soon with spring around the corner. The patent has been registered. It's good to go."

He didn't care anymore. Without Isadora, it meant nothing. Greg was great and very good at his job, but he wasn't Isadora. *Fit to Race*, the race team, the circuit — it all meant nothing now. He'd never put another car on the track, not after what happened in Daytona Beach. The images of that crash — Isadora being lifted out of the car, the damage to her body — it all still haunted his nightmares. He'd wake up in his cabin and look for her, but the space next to him remained empty.

"Has she cashed that check yet?"

Carmelo shook his head. "No."

JT pinched the bridge of his nose. "Jesus, talking to you these days is like pulling teeth. Maybe I should change professions and become your dentist instead."

Carmelo slammed his glass down on the table, the whiskey splashing up the sides of the glass, anger and frustration crawling up his spine. "No, she hasn't cashed the goddamn check. I want you to draw up the papers to sign *Fit to Race* over to her. She'll need something to do now she's not racing anymore."

JT shot to his feet. "Are you out of your ever-loving mind?"

"I don't want any of it anymore. If she won't cash the check, I'll make sure she has something else to secure her financial future. Then I'm taking the yacht and heading out to sea as soon as the house is sold. Joe and I might sail up the coast to Seattle, have a look at a new venture there."

"You are insane. Both of you. I can't believe Joe would let you do this. When will you admit you're in love with her? God damn it, man, don't be a fool. She's miserable without you and you are equally miserable without her. "

"Since when do you care? Not so long ago, you were telling me I was making a mistake getting involved with her. Remember that, JT? The days when we all thought she was Sara Stewart." White hot anger curled in his belly as they faced off.

"That was before I knew she'd been screwed over by Meira who, I am pleased to say, had his sentence handed down to him in court yesterday." JT's jaw was set in that stubborn way that meant he wouldn't be distracted from making his point. "Isadora might want to hear that from you."

"You're her lawyer. She can hear it from you."

The anger dissolved back into the hollow emptiness that had taken hold of him. In his heart, Carmelo wanted to call her, hear her voice, but in his mind he figured she probably didn't want to talk to him.

He'd done what he had to do. Even though any threat of danger to her had passed and the cops had got to Meira before he could get to Carmelo, he'd made too many mistakes with Isadora.

He'd played cat and mouse — sleeping with her then pushing her away, only to pursue her again. Then he'd put her life in danger on the track. He'd never forgive himself for that. She was better off without him in her life, better off thinking that he'd paid her hospital bills and legal fees out of guilt. Far better off cashing her check and starting a new life, even though the thought of her doing so made his heart and his head hurt.

"You're a stubborn, stupid bastard, Carmelo. I'll get those papers drawn up. Don't be surprised if she throws them back at you when we call a meeting to sign them. She won't be happy about this. It's nothing more than another payoff. She'll be insulted and angry."

And that suited him fine. The angrier she was with him — the more unforgiving — the easier it would be to forget that he'd loved her with every fiber of his being. "Good. Make it happen and arrange a meeting." That way he'd get to see her one last time before he closed the door behind her forever. But somewhere deep inside he knew that saying goodbye would be impossible, and if there was even a small chance of her forgiving him, he'd be right back in her arms.

Chapter Twenty-Five

A bitterly cold wind swirled in the Bay. Fall had turned to winter, and San Francisco had weathered the bitter freeze with hot coffee, thick coats, and woolen scarves the way it had for years. Life went on.

Three months had passed since Isadora had returned to her apartment. Her injuries had healed well and the moon boot was due to come off today. The only reminder of what had happened in Daytona Beach would be the scars on her leg and heart.

Between the physiotherapist and Mike, the muscles in her leg and arms would be strong again, but her racing days were over. Wins, losses, the adrenaline of the race — they meant nothing without Carmelo. She'd had offers from other team owners, good ones, but they no longer stirred the passion she'd once had for the sport. Isadora de la Cruz, NASCAR driver, was dead.

Harlon Meira was doing time in San Francisco's State Penitentiary, unlikely to see parole for a long time, and while she hadn't been able to recover the money he'd stolen from her, she was happy justice had been served.

All that haunted her now were the dreams of being in Carmelo's arms, only to wake up and find the bed empty.

"You need to talk to him, Isadora."

Mike held the car door open for her. He'd offered to drive her to her appointment. So had Joe, who'd found out via Greg, but driving with him would only remind Isadora of Carmelo.

"What's the point? I need to get over it and move on."

"He's selling *Fit to Race*."

"It's none of my business what he does."

"You haven't seen him lately. He's pining. For you."

Isadora shrugged. "And I keep telling you, you're a hopeless romantic. Guys like him don't pine. They move on. I'm sure his phone is running hot with offers." The thought that it might be started a nasty green boil in her stomach.

"Greg's fielding hundreds of calls every day," Mike answered dryly and closed the door. He moved around to the driver's side and got in. "Seriously, he's not looking good. Even Joe is worried about him."

"Not my circus, not my monkeys."

"You don't mean that, honey. I mean, look at you. Skinny as a broomstick with great big bags under your eyes."

"And you call yourself my friend. In case you hadn't noticed, I've just been through hell."

"The same one sexy Carmelo's been through." He held up his hands in surrender as Isadora shot him a filthy look. "Just saying ..."

He had a point though. Maybe if she saw Carmelo one more time, she could forget him. She still had his check in her purse. She'd thought to mail it back to him but hadn't quite made it to the post office yet. That was a good enough excuse to go and see him, to give it back. And take one last look before she filed away those dreams forever. She had to move on. If only she had a clue where to.

Her phone rang and she pulled it out of her purse, frowning at the number on the screen. Isadora tapped the screen to answer. "Hello, JT. What's up?"

"Hey, Isadora. Can you come into the office after your doctor's appointment?"

She sighed. What now? Her business with JT had ended when Harlon was convicted of fraud among all the other charges they'd had brought against him. While they hadn't exactly become friends, they'd made their peace with each other. "Why?"

"Carmelo's signing *Fit to Race* over to you."

"What? Is he crazy?" Isadora almost dropped the phone.

"Something like that."

She didn't know whether to agree with him or be insulted. "That's insane, JT. Mike told me he was thinking of selling up. That would be a much better option. I don't want anything from him. And even if I did, I have no idea how to run a business that size. That's professional suicide."

"He feels guilty for what happened to you. He's determined that it's his fault for keeping you on to race at Daytona Beach. He thinks this is the next best step for you if you choose not to go back into racing."

"Well, then he *is* crazy. I want nothing from him."

"I've tried to talk him out of it, but he won't listen to me. Maybe he'll listen to you."

"Damn straight I'll make him listen." Annoyance simmered. She was tired of being manipulated and didn't need yet another reminder of Carmelo in her life. Nothing would make her sign those papers. "I'll ask Mike if he can run me in." She looked over at Mike and he nodded. "I'll be there right after my appointment."

"Thanks, Isadora." The relief in his voice echoed down the line.

Two hours later, she marched into the outer office as fast as her limp would allow. Her leg felt strange without the weight of the boot and the twinge of pain from the newly healed bones slowed her down. The surgeon had assured her that once she'd regained full muscle strength, she'd lose the worst of the limp. Thankfully, the fracture had healed well.

Greg stood to greet her, pressing a kiss onto each of her cheeks. Her annoyance had abated but irritation remained.

"Are they in there?" She waved a hand at the door.

"Only Carmelo is, love. Be careful, he's a tad snarly."

"Good. Just the way I want it because I'm a tad snarly too." She took off her coat and thrust it into Mike's hands. "Hold this for me, would you?"

Without bothering to knock, she pushed Carmelo's office door open, marched in and closed it firmly behind her. She wouldn't put it past Greg and Mike to have their ears to the wood.

Her heart shuddered at the sight of Carmelo where he sat on the sofa, his tie loose, the two top buttons undone on his shirt and a rerun of the Daytona Beach race playing on the television screen on the wall. Her gaze glued to the screen as the accident unfolded before her. Seeing it happen from the outside was almost as scary as it had been on the inside. It made her feel lucky to be alive.

Isadora drew in a sharp breath as she watched her car flip through the air and land on the roof, remembered the bone-shattering pain she'd endured as it skidded across the grass.

Carmelo looked up and she caught a glimpse of tiredness etched into the lines fanning out from his eyes and the crease of his forehead. He'd grown a beard, perhaps not intentionally, more like he'd forgotten to shave or couldn't be bothered to. On him the look was as sexy as hell.

His gaze returned to the screen. "Every time I watch it, I think how I could have killed you."

Isadora barely heard his words above the video commentary but the hollow ring in his tone made her heart ache. How on earth had she ever thought she could get over him? "You didn't try to kill me. Harlon did."

Carmelo shook his head. "I should never have let you race on after Phoenix. I should never have let you race at all." He pulled off his tie and tossed it onto a folder on the coffee table in front of the sofa.

Isadora stepped forward to stand in front of the screen, blocking his view. He picked up the remote and turned it off. Opening her purse, she pulled out the envelope and held it out to him. He looked at it, knowing full well what it was, the company name printed in bold red lettering in the top left-hand corner, but didn't reach out to take it.

"Your check. I don't want it and I don't want *Fit to Race*."

"I don't want them either."

"Fine." She tore the envelope into tiny pieces and tossed them onto the coffee table, watching them flutter down like confetti. "Hand me that contract and I'll do the same."

He leaned forward, elbows on his thighs, and rested his forehead on his fists. His hair had grown, curling into his nape like a lover's touch. Her hands itched to touch him. It disappointed her that he seemed to have no fight left in him.

"I don't understand why you want me to have it." She rested her fists on her hips.

"Because you need something to do that doesn't involve you being thrown around like a crash test dummy."

"You don't get to make that choice for me. Especially not after three months of silence."

"God damn it, Isadora!" He stood; tall, dark, and angry. "You could have died out there."

Isadora stood her ground as he strode around the coffee table to stop in front of her. In her ballet flats, he towered over her, all broad shoulders, wide chest, and tapered waist. He'd lost weight as she had and the bags under his eyes suggested he was getting as little sleep as she was. At least his eyes had some life in them now she'd stirred some emotion in him.

"But I didn't. And you have nothing to feel guilty about."

"Harlon Meira—"

"Is in jail where he belongs, serving a long sentence for embezzlement and conspiracy to cause bodily harm, with a few other charges tacked on. I'd like to see him serve a harsher sentence, but he got what was coming to him in the end."

"You know what hurt the most?"

Isadora raised an eyebrow. "Gee, I don't know. Hitting the wall? The rollover? Getting T-boned? Spinning out of control?"

He closed his eyes, his skin pale as she reminded him of what she'd been through. "No, that's not what I meant, but I wish it hadn't happened to you." He placed his hands on her shoulders. She'd expected them to be warm but instead they were ice cold through the silky material of her blouse. He opened his eyes and looked right into hers, his gaze all pain and guilt mixed with self-loathing. "It hurt that you would think I was capable of cheating and then trying to pay you off."

"It's what I was led to believe. How could I have known anything different? I was as much a victim as you were. I didn't know you then like I know you now." She lifted a hand to his face. "The man I know wouldn't be beaten by this. He'd get back out there, launch that damn clothing range, and rebuild that car."

"No amount of cloth protection could have saved you from injury out there."

"Look how far we've come since the early days. There are way fewer deaths or serious injury on the track now because of innovators like you. *Fit to Race* needs you, not me."

"*Fit to Race* needs both of us, or no one at all. I nearly lost you." He ran his palms down her arms to take her hands in his. "When they got you out of that car and you weren't moving—" He shook his head. "Then when I found out Meira was coming after me next, I realized you weren't safe with me. If he found us together, he'd have no hesitation in finishing what he'd started at the track and hurt you again too."

"And that's why I didn't see you again until I was discharged from the hospital?"

"I had to end it with you. I couldn't bear to see you hurt again."

"So you let JT handle it like the big brave man you are." She wanted to stay angry with him, but his thumbs moved across the back of her hands sending red hot signals through her blood that made her knees weak.

"This thing between us, I don't understand it. I've never felt about anyone the way I feel about you."

Her heart skipped several beats as he lifted her hands to his lips. She forgot all about coming to his office to finish it and wanted to start something instead. She understood now why he'd walked away only to be lured back again. Without each other they were both lost. His hands moved to her hips to draw her closer and she let him.

"I love you, Isadora. But I'd rather be without you than see you hurt again."

Her hands curled into the fabric of his shirt. "I won't be. Because if I can't have you, none of it means anything. I'm done with racing for good. These past few months have been awful without you. I love you and I want to be where you are. It hurt me to think that you were only doing what you did for me out of a need to protect yourself. Or worse, out of pity."

"Everything I did for you in Daytona Beach, I did because I wanted to. I hated that you thought I'd done it for any other reason."

"I was angry with you for abandoning me. I felt used. And then when you let JT do all the talking and left without a word, I thought you didn't want me anymore."

"If I'd opened my mouth that day, all the wrong things would have come out of it. JT didn't want to take any chances after what happened on the yacht." His arms came around her and anchored her body against his.

She pressed her face into his chest. What a fool she'd been. "I'm so sorry." She inhaled the heady scent she'd come to associate with Carmelo — the clean, spicy smell of his cologne as it radiated with every pulse of his heart. She knew that more than anything else in the world, she wanted him beside her.

He tipped her chin up with his forefinger. "Stay with me. Let me make it up to you. If you don't want *Fit to Race,* I'll sell it. Or we can run it together. Either way, I don't think I could hold onto it another day if you're not there to share it with me. Can we start over?"

"I think I'd like that."

His mouth descended to hers, his lips soft, warm, and coaxing. She kissed him back, in no hurry to speed things up. She wanted to savor every moment because in his embrace, she'd come home.

THE END

About the Author

Finding love and hope in small country
towns with dark secrets ....

Juanita escapes the real world by reading and writing Australian Rural Romance novels with elements of suspense, Australian Fantasy Paranormal and Small Town USA stories. Her romance novels star spirited heroines who give the hero a run for his money before giving in. She creates emotionally engaging worlds steeped in romance, suspense, mystery and intrigue, set in dusty, rural outback Australia and on the NASCAR racetracks of America.

Her small town USA and Australian rural romances have made the Amazon bestseller and top 100 lists. Juanita writes mostly contemporary and Australian rural romantic suspense but also likes to dabble in the ponds of fantasy and paranormal with Greek gods brought to life in the 21st century. When she's not writing, Juanita is mother to three boys and has a passion for fast cars and country living.

Author Site: juanitakees.com

Goodreads: Juanita_Kees

BookBub: juanita-kees

Other Books By Juanita Kees

Whispers at Wongan Creek

Secrets at Wongan Creek

Shadows over Wongan Creek

Under Shadow of Doubt

Under the Hood

Under Cover of Dark

Montana Baby

Montana Daughter

Montana Son

The Gods of Oakleigh

Home to Bindarra Creek

Promise Me Forever